THE MONSTER IN THE LOCH

BY

ALANNA KNIGHT

CB

CONTEMPORARY BOOKS

a division of NTC/CONTEMPORARY PUBLISHING GROUP
Lincolnwood, Illinois USA

 Thumbprint
Mysteries

MORE THUMBPRINT MYSTERIES

by Alanna Knight:

The Royal Park Murder
Dead Beckoning

This is a work of fiction. The characters, incidents, and dialogues are products of the author's imagination and are not to be construed as real. Any resemblance to actual events or persons, living or dead, is entirely coincidental.

Cover Illustration: Gerard Dubois

ISBN: 0-8092-0688-9

Published by Contemporary Books,
a division of NTC/Contemporary Publishing Group, Inc.,
4255 West Touhy Avenue,
Lincolnwood (Chicago), Illinois 60646-1975 U.S.A.

890 QB 0 9 8 7 6 5 4 3 2 1

CHAPTER 1

The day it all went wrong and Dad fell and broke his ankle began like a thousand others. Things were very quiet in Hamish Kelty's bookshop on the Royal Mile. There was nothing to hint at danger. Or to suggest that I was to leave Edinburgh on a journey of terror.

I'm Hamish's daughter Annie, and I can't recall having more than three customers in the shop at a time. If we did, I guess the police would think we had an unlawful gathering.

We don't sell porn or romances—just students' textbooks and some rare editions of classics by well-known authors that Dad considers an important luxury. Since buyers for the classics are even rarer than the books themselves, the university books for various courses pay the rent and keep a roof over our heads. The students, God bless them, provide our daily bread.

Dad is also a courier of rare and precious items for special clients, a secret trade I know little about. My boyfriend Calum the Cop, as Dad still calls him, says Dad "plays his cards close to his chest." I've known Dad twenty-four years longer than Calum has, and I think Dad often comes close to breaking the law on some shady deals.

I also suspect that Calum shares my feelings but he's too polite. He pretends it's all sweetness and light where his future father-in-law is concerned.

So by mutual consent we never discuss Dad's business deals that take him away from Edinburgh for a few days—deals he never talks about when he comes home. In the past if I have dared to ask, his reply has been that clients relied on his keeping quiet. Part of the deal was that he would never discuss it with anyone. Not even his daughter.

Once my curiosity got the better of me and nearly ended in disaster. A former partner of Dad's was found murdered in the Royal Park at Holyrood Palace, and Dad was suspect number one. The fact that I proved he didn't do it by tracking down the real killer has given me a taste for crime detection.

I liked the idea of being a private eye and could see a whole new exciting and dangerous world opening up. A world I was very anxious to explore a little further before I became Mrs. Calum Crail and settled down to a life of domestic bliss and babies.

Besides, I still had one major mystery in my own life to solve. The riddle of my nonexistent mother. Dad wouldn't talk about her. All I knew was that I had been four years old when she vanished from our lives. I feared that I had played some vital role in whatever tragedy had happened.

Dad wouldn't discuss this with me. Maybe this was

"the grief that lay too deep for tears." On the other hand, it could be because he loved me. He didn't want to ruin my life and my future with the truth—the truth I aimed to discover before I married Calum.

Calum didn't know this, of course. It would have been bad news for him. Dad pretended to him that my mother was dead. Calum is very sympathetic whenever the subject is hinted at. Calum has no idea of the secret fear that has never left me—a fear that I will never confess to any living person and hardly admit to myself. Sometimes I can push it aside for a while, but then the nightmare comes back.

In those witches' hours when a wind howls down the old chimneys, when the ghosts of old Edinburgh swirl about the cobblestones beneath my bedroom window, I am really scared. If I could tear aside the veil over the past, then I might see that I had caused her death in some dreadful manner. And I would know that Dad's only wish is to protect me from learning the truth.

And so the mystery of my mother has to be solved. It goes on the secret list of things to do before I get married.

This story, however, begins on the day when Dad fell downstairs. No one would call what happened a disaster. Dad is a big, strong man—very healthy. But a broken ankle is a little awkward when you live on the fourth floor of a historic house with a spiral staircase. And seventy steps up from your bookshop on ground level! If you forget something, you are in no great hurry to go back for it.

Anyway, Dad's injury, as I've said, was not severe but its timing was awful.

It had come in the midst of one of his big deals. A valuable goblet was to be delivered to a buyer in the

Highlands. According to Dad, the goblet once belonged to Mary, Queen of Scots. Indeed, there is a painting in the Portrait Gallery by a court painter of the time. It shows Mary kneeling in her private chapel in Holyrood Palace and receiving the sacrament from what looks like the same cup.

I wasn't sure I believed the story until I saw with my own eyes the picture hanging there. Calum went with me. We both decided the goblet was probably genuine.

So Dad had a goblet to deliver. Couldn't it wait?

No, was the answer. The seller was quite definite. There was a buyer waiting for an immediate sale.

"What about sending it by special mail delivery?" I asked.

"No, Annie, it's far too precious for that," Dad replied. As were most items in Dad's courier deals. They had to be delivered by hand from seller to buyer, no middlemen or mail service whatever. All this special handling made me think that Dad often handled "delicate" or stolen goods.

"You are the only one I can trust, Annie. There's big money in this for us. It will all go towards your dowry," he added, hoping that would impress me.

When I sighed, he said, "Heaven knows we need the money." He then went into a long detail of how much we had in the bank, and even the bits I understood, which weren't many, turned me pale. It sounded as if we were being faced with ruin and only the safe delivery of the goblet could save us.

"There's a dealer over from the States," Dad continued, "staying at the castle—"

"Wait a moment—did you say *castle*?"

"Yes, Castle Roy. Near the shores of Loch Ness."

"Loch Ness—with the monster?"

Dad smiled. "I'll show you." Opening a map of Scotland, he spread it out on the table. "Castle Roy has its own loch—Loch Roy—and its own monster—whatever that is. Don't you remember reading about it a little while ago?"

"Of course. And it was on television. Two people in a boat disappeared. The boat drifted ashore but the people were never found."

"Correct. And that revived the old monster theory. According to the geologists, Loch Roy was once joined to Loch Ness. There's a thin stretch of land between them now. The theory is that perhaps Nessie left a brother or sister monster behind in Loch Roy."

I was impressed. In fact, I was beginning to like the idea of a visit to a Highland castle to deliver Queen Mary's precious goblet in person.

"Tell me about Castle Roy, Dad. Who lives there now?"

"The present owners are very poor indeed. Their name is Stuart—like a lot of other people in Scotland, whichever way it is spelled. They claim a blood link with the royal House of Stuart and collect anything to do with Queen Mary, or Bonnie Prince Charlie, or the Jacobites."

He shook his head sadly. "There are locks of the Prince's hair and pieces from his tartan kilt in so many castles, I suspect he must have gone out to fight the English bald and stark naked.

"As for Queen Mary's gloves," Dad went on warming to his pet subject, "it seems she was a very careless lady. She left one glove in every stately home she visited. An expensive business, since embroidered gloves were strictly for the nobility. As for the number of beds she slept in, well, she can't have had many nights at home in her own bed here in Holyrood Palace."

"You were telling me about the Stuarts at Castle Roy," I reminded him gently.

"Well, they have quite a lot of interesting historic antiques, and they are desperate for ready cash. They take in tourists as a money-making scheme. Bed, breakfast, and a banquet-style dinner in the Great Hall, all served up with bagpipes, whisky, and a big dose of family history and ancestors. Besides Europeans and Americans, people named Stuart visit from all over the world. Even the occasional Japanese has been known to arrive on the doorstep."

Dad sighed. "They make their money in the summer when the Highlands and the weather are at their best. The moors all purple heather with deer and a few birds to shoot. That provides for the long cold winter when they have to wear their overcoats indoors to keep warm."

He smiled. "Old castles weren't built for comfort. They're drafty places! I hope I'm not putting you off, Annie. Do you still want to go?"

"Try and stop me! When do I leave?"

Scotland isn't a big country. To make a delivery to a castle two hundred miles northwest of Edinburgh doesn't sound like any big deal, except that neither Dad nor I drive. Dad did once upon a time, but he lost his license long ago. He has told several different stories of how this came about. But my guess is that it was one drink too many, too many times.

I never learned to drive because we live in the center of the city where owning a car is more of a problem than a pleasure. There are so many narrow, twisting one-way streets and no-parking areas. Not having a car has never bothered us, however, as most places are in easy walking distance of the Royal Mile. And there are plenty of taxis, buses, and trains. Train was the way I would travel to Castle Roy. .

I went down to the local travel agent and we consulted timetables.

"The railway runs up here to Inverness," the girl pointed on the map. "Your castle is—here, but you'll have to leave the train at Glenmohr—here—and take a bus to Loch Roy."

She paused and shook her head. "The roads are pretty poor at the moment, but with this sighting of a monster in the loch maybe things will improve," she added hopefully. "There's nothing like a Nessie rumor for bringing in extra busloads of tourists during the summer vacation season and when the grouse shooting starts."

I was looking at the map. "Lochroy village is just across the water from Glenmohr."

She laughed. "Exactly—just over the hills as the crow flies. But it's nearer twenty kilometers by road. You have to go right around the loch."

Since I wasn't a crow and there were hills and a loch in the way of my two legs, I would have to find some other way.

The travel agent pulled out a dog-eared timetable. "Don't worry. We'll get you there. That's our business," she said cheerfully. "You leave the train at Glenmohr and take the local school bus to Lochroy village. There are only two buses a day, one in the morning to take the kids to Glenmohr and one in the afternoon to take them home again."

When I explained all this to Calum, he said, "I have some vacation time. We'll go on the motorcycle. We can cut across the hills—no bother. Besides autumn's a great time of year in the Highlands. You'll love it, Annie."

Calum had solved the problem and that sounded great to me. I was very interested in the nights we might spend in romantic old hotels with four-poster beds.

When we told Dad, he nearly had a fit. I thought at first he was doing the heavy father, being prim about the correct way engaged couples on vacation should behave. Then I realized that his concern was for the goblet. No way would he trust his precious antique to a motorcycle ride across the Highlands.

"If you still had your car, I might have considered it," he added firmly and that was his final word on the subject.

Calum sighed deeply. When he was promoted, they let him have the squad car. Officially it was for police duty only. One of his friends made him a good offer for his own car, and Calum bought a motorcycle. I wasn't pleased, but I guess he had always secretly longed for a motorcycle.

"Don't worry, Annie," Calum said. "I'll borrow my brother Sean's car for a couple of days. Just you leave it to me. And we'll be able to take Nero along with us." He grinned. "Mum will be glad to get him out of the house for a while."

Nero was Calum's new pet—a very large, very fierce dog with a huge appetite. I suppose it went with Calum's macho image, motorcycle and all.

Nero was the latest addition to the Crail family. He was an Alsatian ex-police dog who had seen years of active service as a sniffer-dog with the drug squad. In armed combat with one of the dealers, his leg had been broken. He would have been destroyed, but Detective Sergeant Calum Crail saved him from the firing squad in the nick of time!

So Calum took Nero home, warned that he needed a lot of food and a lot of exercise. The Royal Park nearby was a doggy heaven with heathery slopes and hills to climb. So I got more than my fair share of exercise with Calum and Nero in all kinds of weather.

However, I suspected that Nero was one reason why Calum's mother was so eager to put forward our wedding date. He took up too much room, she complained. And for a home-loving, house-proud Mum, he smelled too—especially when his coat got wet.

Worst of all, he didn't share Mrs. Crail's passion for babies. In fact, she confided in me one day that she didn't like the way he looked at the grandchildren, especially the tiny ones. "I've seen him licking his lips, Annie," she whispered. "Exactly like a nicer kind of dog would look at a juicy bone."

Nero scared me witless but Calum tried to calm my fears. He insisted that Nero was a big, soft dog, gentle as a lamb. The thought of driving through the Highlands with Nero in the backseat, breathing down my neck, filled me with some very gloomy thoughts indeed. In fact, if I had to choose between Nero and the Loch Roy monster, I would have had a hard time deciding!

But Fate had another plan in mind—even more beastly!

CHAPTER 2

With no idea of what the future had in store, I prepared to leave for the Highlands, the guardian of a precious goblet. The more I thought about that drive of two hundred miles with Calum and Nero, the less I liked the idea.

I've always been terrified of anything on four legs larger than a squirrel. Calum was amazed that I was terrified of Nero. The dog became the only source of trouble between us.

When I winced at this superdog charging toward me, claws scraping the ground, tongue lolling over large white teeth, Dad was sympathetic. He explained to Calum that I had been attacked and knocked over by a black Labrador when I was a small girl.

"She never got over it. She used to scream when she saw a dog on the other side of the street, even on a leash," Dad said, shaking his head sadly.

"She'll get over it with Nero," said Calum firmly. "He loves people—he's so gentle. She'll learn to trust him and have him eating out of her hand in no time."

So it seemed that this was to be the first great test. If I wanted Calum and a car to go to the Highlands, then Nero must come too.

It was all fixed, but then Fate stepped in. Calum's vacation was canceled. An unexpected visit to Holyrood Palace by a European head of state. This VIP was to be met and entertained by a member of the royal family. Calum was on escort duty.

He groaned. "If you can wait just a few days, Annie."

Dad called Castle Roy and came back shaking his head. "There's just no way the date can be changed. The buyer has to be in Paris for a business deal. I'm afraid Annie will have to go on her own."

And to me he said, "Nothing to worry about, Annie. It's an easy journey. They'll meet you with a car when you get arrive in Lochroy. Just call them from the phone when you get off the bus."

It sounded simple enough. I did rather like the idea of that train and bus journey. I could catch up on my reading too. Although I would miss Calum, what bliss not to have Nero perched in the backseat!

"I just hope it doesn't snow," said Susie gloomily. Susie is our neighbor across the road who is quite fond of Dad. The weatherman is her daytime favorite on television. "The forecast is very bad today, Annie. Heavy rain, sleet, and snow on high ground."

"Have a heart, Susie. We're still in October."

She shook her head. "You have to be prepared. You just never know in that part of the world. The Highlands are well known for their rain."

I should have been used to it by now. Susie usually began predicting a white Christmas at the end of September. I didn't like to spoil Susie's gloomy enjoyment, but I really like winter in Edinburgh. It can be quite magical. With the castle and our ancient houses twisting down the Royal Mile, all snowcapped, the frosty air is like wine. For a few brief days, the city is the setting for a fairy tale.

I had no illusions, however, about winter in the Highlands. A sudden snowfall can be a killer in the mountains. In isolated villages, roads cease to exist, motorists get stranded, animals and people die. A sudden storm is nothing short of disaster. You can forget all about modern progress and central heating when you have to go back to candles. Houses no longer have proper chimneys and fireplaces to boil the kettle on.

So thanking Susie for her warning, I promised to pack warm clothes and gave her my blessing. I guess she was looking forward to getting me out of the way and having Dad all to herself for a few days.

Susie's mother owns the bakery across the road. She was willing—even eager—to let Susie help Dad in the shop. I guess Mrs. Main saw Hamish Kelty as husband material. Having Susie take care of all his needs was a gift from heaven—the answer to all a mother's prayers for a pretty, thirty-ish, single daughter.

So I didn't feel in the least guilty about leaving. Susie would spoil Dad rotten and they'd both enjoy every minute together. To be honest, I agreed with Mrs. Main. I thought Susie would be a super wife for Dad and a great stepmother.

*   *   *

The train station was only five minutes' walk down Market Street so off I went, armed with tickets, map, the goblet, and Dad's last-minute instructions. Susie came with me, insisting that she must see me safely onto the train. When she thrust a chocolate bar, a Coke, and a magazine into my hands, I felt quite touched. I felt as if I were off on a mission to a headhunting tribe in the Amazon instead of the Scottish Highlands.

I'd rather hoped Calum might be waiting on the platform too. However, there were already great crowds swirling round Princes Street waiting for a glimpse of royalty. I guessed he would be somewhere among them on official duty.

Nero would be with him, just to keep the crowd in order and scare any children into hysterics who got out of line. Soft and gentle, indeed!

"You're not taking much, are you?" said Susie. She cannot leave home for even one night without a huge suitcase and three different outfits for every occasion.

She eyed the small backpack I was wearing. Neat and comfortable, it was my favorite luggage. It was large enough for survival kit, camera, and the small necessities of life. All were now squeezed in alongside a small wooden box containing the goblet, a print of the Queen Mary painting, and copies of the documents the buyer would produce at Castle Roy to prove his identity.

"I've packed an extra sweater and warm socks," I told Susie.

"Are you sure that's enough?"

"It is for me for a couple of days," I said firmly.

Susie shook her head. "And what if there's a smart cocktail party or dinner at the castle? Like we see on TV," she added hopefully. "Scottish dancing and the like."

I shrugged. "So what if there is?"

She looked at my jeans, leather jacket, boots, and woolly hat.

"Oh, Annie," she wailed. "You do look exactly like a hitchhiker."

"Not to worry," I said. "I have the little black dress tucked away for emergencies." I wasn't sure that she believed me.

At that moment the train began to move. We left Susie standing there on the platform looking as if she'd been left over from a Forties movie like *Brief Encounter*.

"See you on Thursday," I sang out as the door was closing.

She sniffed sadly. Susie liked to get every ounce of drama out of a situation. If she'd owned white linen hankies instead of boxes of Kleenex, I swear she would have had one crisp and clean, all ready to wave farewell like we see in old movies.

The train was *The Flying Scotsman*, traveling from London to Inverness. I found my reserved seat. It was one of four with a table, useful for leaning books and elbows on. I put down my book and a magazine. There was a long journey ahead, and it would be pretty quiet with few other people in the train car.

The seat opposite with a reserved ticket was vacant. I wondered where the traveler was and whether he would be fascinating. Notice I say *he*, not *she*. I have to confess that I do share some of Susie's romantic ideas. I have to agree with her that trains provide more chances of meeting exciting strangers than airplanes do.

Suddenly all my speculation about the missing traveler was at an end.

An elderly gentleman with longish gray hair and spectacles sat down opposite. He was carrying an important-looking red leather case. It was larger than a briefcase, the kind a Cabinet minister might have carried. However, I decided that his clothes weren't smart enough for a businessman or a government official. Anyway, they would have traveled first class.

But that briefcase was old and well-cared for. My powers of deduction went to work on it. The man was probably a college professor and the case was a treasured possession from his student days.

I was curious about him. Why was he so out of breath? As if he had been running for the train and almost missed it. Yet the reserved notice on his seat said he came from London. Maybe he had a heart condition, I thought, standing up to put my jacket on the luggage rack. As he snapped open the case, I saw that it was lined with faded velvet. There was a coat of arms and gold initials.

As I sat down again, he was already spreading his papers across the table. He made no apology for taking up so much room. I felt a little resentful at having my space invaded like this, but I soon got over it.

Despite Susie's gloomy weather report, I looked out the train's windows at a beautiful day. The sun shone in a cloudless sky, and the fields were like a great rainbow-colored quilt. The woods were ablaze with autumn-colored red and yellow trees; every hedgerow was blue and mauve. And we were never out of sight of a horizon of rich purple hills.

My paperback was a crime novel by a popular young Scottish writer. I had been saving it for the journey, but I found my attention wandering. I am like that on train journeys. I can't bear to miss a moment of the scenery.

And just for good measure, as we sped through tiny hamlets and the hills folded themselves around us, I saw a deer herd. They had come down to drink by a stream. Then a fox, his coat bright red against the yellow stubble of the fields, was alerted by the train's approach. He raced across a field and leaped over a stone wall. Birds there were too, a great black army of crows wheeling against the sky.

Pure magic! I was just sorry I had no one to share it all with. I sometimes looked hopefully at my companion, although that word hardly described him. Certainly the joy

I felt at this amazing countryside did not touch him as he frowned over his papers. He was writing furiously, pausing to throw down his pen with a gasp of annoyance. He had fixed his briefcase to shield his papers from my gaze. As if I could read them upside down! My curiosity was aroused, however, and by stretching my neck a little, I noticed that he was dealing with columns of figures and symbols.

Why on earth didn't he use a portable computer to do his work for him, like most folks in this day and age?

I enjoy trying to guess about people when I sit opposite them in buses or meet them in supermarket lines. Train travel gives an even better chance to study fellow travelers. So who was this man I had labeled at first glance as a professor? Where was he going and why were those papers causing him so much trouble?

His only distraction was when our car door slid open. He glanced nervously over his shoulder. Were we both waiting for the refreshments trolley and hopeful for a cup of coffee? Or was it something more sinister in his case? I couldn't explain how, but I felt fear reaching out from him across the table.

Putting aside my book, I decided to have a coffee and get rid of my silly thoughts! Although we hadn't engaged in any talk, I stood up and said politely, "I don't think there's a coffee service on this train." Pointing at his wildly scattered papers, I asked, "May I bring you something back from the dining car?"

He seemed aware of me for the first time. He blinked, confused for a moment, and then he smiled. "That's mighty kind of you, miss. I'd surely be most grateful."

Digging into his jacket pocket, he took out a wallet and handed me a five-pound note. "Please, I need some change. Perhaps you'd bring me back a burger. I haven't eaten since I boarded the train this morning. And I guess we've still quite some distance to go."

When I told him the time of the train's arrival at Inverness, he frowned and shook his head. "I'm only going as far as—Glenmohr, is it?"

"So am I," I said. "Yes, we should be there in about an hour."

He looked startled. "As long as that? I had no idea." And frowning again, he went back to his papers.

No doubt he was too busy to look at timetables. This problem he was working out must be very difficult indeed. From the few words we had exchanged, he sounded American. So where were the laptop computer and the mobile telephone most important travelers carried with them on trains?

I warmed to him then. In some ways he reminded me of Dad, who would be like that too—forgetting all about eating, still working out sums on bits of paper.

Now that I had broken the ice, our journey should make some interesting conversation when I came back from the dining car. I wondered what kind of business might be taking a professor to a remote village in the Highlands.

Before leaving my seat, I put on my backpack.

The professor looked up from his papers and pointed to it. "I'll look after that for you, if you like."

When I shook my head and said, "Thanks for the offer, anyway," he gave me a strange look.

As I walked along three cars in the swaying train to the dining car, wearing my backpack, I felt rather embarrassed. I should have left it with him since my action hinted that I didn't trust him.

Afterwards, as things turned out, I was to be very glad I had obeyed my instincts and taken it with me.

CHAPTER
3

I joined a long line at the dining car. It looked as if all the passengers on the train had decided at the same moment that they were hungry. They all wanted more than just coffee. The orders were for burgers or other cooked snacks. With only one microwave and one man serving, we were in for a long wait.

Meanwhile, the train had stopped at a small station. Among the few backpackers who got aboard were two men in business suits. They went up and down the platform, walking fast and unable to conceal their anxiety.

The second time they peered into the window, I decided they were either meeting someone off the train or searching for the car with their reserved seats. They didn't look the types who would book seats from a remote station along the line. The first-class section was mostly empty since it was no longer tourist season. And if the car I had left was an example, they could have found seats anywhere on the train.

Five minutes later, clutching a paper carrier with hamburger and two cups of coffee, I staggered back along the train. As we got deeper into the Highlands, the track twisted and turned. As our speed dropped, the swaying of the cars got worse. There was nothing the railway company could do to provide long, straight stretches of track when the landscape was all mountains and streams. However, it was a very pleasant way to travel.

At last I reached my car all ready to apologize for the long delay. But the professor was nowhere to be seen.

For a moment I looked around and wondered if I had taken the wrong direction. The dining car is in the middle of the train. Had I gone north instead of south?

But there were our reserved tickets, mine from Edinburgh and the professor's from London. My paperback was where I had left it, but his part of the table had been cleared. I looked around and decided he had gone to the toilet. Had I been away such a long time he thought I wasn't coming back? And that I had gone off with his five-pound note?

According to Susie, I looked like a scruffy hitchhiker. If she was right, the professor had every reason for not wishing to leave his precious papers on the table. The railways put up warning notices: Never leave luggage unattended! No doubt the professor, who wasn't even English, had heard plenty of tales about stolen belongings. Perhaps he had his own reasons for not trusting me.

After all, I had not been willing to leave my backpack in his custody. That might have made him suspicious.

I sat down and put his coffee and hamburger on the table. It wasn't my business—why should I care what had happened to a complete stranger? We hadn't exchanged more than a dozen words. But I would have liked to restore his good faith in me.

By the time I had drunk my coffee, the two men I had seen boarding the train had walked through the car twice. My curiosity was aroused. Now they were carefully examining the reserved tickets on the backs of the seats. Obviously they hadn't booked seats because they returned a few minutes later. It would take that long, I reckoned, to walk the whole length of the train.

It was then I realized that they weren't looking for seats. They were searching for someone. I studied the moving landscape, pretending to ignore them.

"Excuse me, miss." The younger of the two, a big, burly fellow with a pockmarked face and a boxer's broken nose, leaned across the table. He pointed to the empty seat. "Someone sitting there?"

I nodded vaguely and studied my magazine as if my life depended on reading the next sentence.

The older man moved into my line of vision. Middle-aged, he looked a little frayed at the edges, with dandruff on the collar of his suit and greasy hair.

"Did you hear what we asked you, miss?" His voice was not unpleasant, but there was something threatening about his manner. I decided I didn't like the look of either of them.

Suddenly, as they were carefully studying the reserved ticket on the professor's seat, I guessed they were looking for him. A lot of thoughts came tumbling into my mind.

They were up to no good. He didn't want to see them. Was that why he had disappeared? We hadn't stopped at another station since the men had boarded the train, and I hadn't seen anyone leave the train as I stood at the dining-car window. So the missing professor must still be on the train, keeping out of the way, hiding from these two.

I made up my mind in that instant that they were crooks. I could almost hear Calum's mocking voice when

I told him of my amazing deductions. "It wasn't very much to go on, Annie. Not very valid reasons for suspicions. Dandruff? And a boxer's nose?"

But the idea was there, firmly fixed. Once I got an idea I hung onto it in the face of all evidence. I prided myself that this was the reason I had saved my dad from jail for a murder he didn't commit.

"And very nearly got yourself killed in the process," would be Calum's comment.

This was different. This was just a harmless exercise in observation and deduction to while away the time. It had nothing to do with me personally, I told myself.

I was soon to find out how wrong that was. The two men were standing very still, looking down at me in a very unpleasant manner.

I faced them blankly, trying to pretend they were just chatting and I didn't care for their intentions. But suddenly I was aware that all this was happening in an empty car. I thought of the dangers—

I was dead scared!

"Who's sitting here, miss?" asked the young guy.

I pointed to the reserved ticket. "As you can see, the seat is taken."

"That's not what I asked you." His scowling face said it all—that he'd like to wring this stupid girl's neck.

"This food—" he pointed.

"Is mine," I said, pulling it toward me. "If you want something to eat, there's a dining car three cars back—"

The young guy leaned forward. For a moment I thought he was going to hit me. Then the older guy put a hand on his arm. It said plainer than words: Cool it.

He sat down opposite me in the professor's seat and

smiled pleasantly. "I see you got on at Edinburgh, miss. Was there someone sitting there then? Someone who had got on at London?"

Under the table I crossed my fingers and prepared a lie. I shrugged. "Who knows? Perhaps someone decided against sharing a table. There are plenty of empty ones around, as you can see," I reminded them gently.

"Were you supposed to be meeting someone on the train, miss? Someone who had a seat already?" the older man asked.

I looked from one to the other. "Of course I wasn't. What on earth gave you that idea? And what business is it of yours even if I was?" I sounded calm enough but I was mad. "If you don't leave me alone, I'll have to summon the conductor—"

That did the trick.

"Let's go," said the young guy with an angry look in my direction. "We're just wasting time."

His pal spared a moment to spread a little greasy charm. "Thank you, miss, for your help." Whatever his present occupation, I felt he might have been an actor at some time.

Thankfully, at that moment the announcer over the intercom told us that the train would be arriving in Glenmohr in a few moments. Passengers were reminded to make sure they took all their luggage with them, etc., etc.

The two men looked at each other and set off at a fast pace, heading down the train.

As it shuddered to a halt and I was collecting my things, including the hamburger, which was to come in very useful later, I dropped my magazine. Bending down to pick it up, I noticed an envelope and a sheet of paper under the professor's seat.

"Dr. Z Parker, FRS, PO Box 35, Oxford."

I stood with them in my hand. I imagined him watching the two men walking up the platform, saw him hastily gathering all his papers together—

The envelope was empty. The paper looked like a old map, and there were geometric signs spread over it with numbers and letters. I put them in my pocket.

The professor had told me he was leaving the train at Glenmohr. I'd see him on the platform and hand over the papers along with the money I owed him. I was the first out, but he was nowhere to be seen among the few other passengers who got off the train.

Neither were the two men who I believed were searching for him. Maybe they were traveling on to Inverness. But I couldn't get rid of that uneasy feeling that there was something wrong. The professor had said he was leaving the train at Glenmohr, and I knew there wasn't another stop until Inverness.

Was he a magician? How had he managed to keep out of their way? And what puzzled me even more, how had he left the platform without being seen?

Well, there was a mystery here but one I was never likely to solve. Something more to discuss with Calum when I got home. Another piece of detection, the kind of puzzle he'd have lots of ideas about what really happened. He'd see the details I had missed.

Sometimes I missed my Calum the Cop of the old days on the Royal Mile. Being a plainclothes detective had changed him, or was it because he was so good-looking and even sexier somehow in his old uniform?

I certainly wished he was with me. It was only a day since we parted, but I already missed him as if it had been weeks ago. I would have even welcomed Nero trotting alongside.

I looked around. There wasn't much to Glenmohr, a Highland village, with one long, gray main street, a church, and a school. A few houses and small farms were scattered on the hillside beyond. But all my thoughts were on catching the country school bus. According to the travel agent in Edinburgh, it waited briefly in the station square en route to Lochroy. Once there, all I had to do was phone from the village, and the Stuarts' car would be on its way to collect me.

Dad had arranged it all. "It's a long walk up the drive to the castle," they had warned him.

I looked around the square and panicked. Where was the bus? The train had arrived five minutes late. Had the bus left on time? If I had missed it, then I'd have to wait until tomorrow at the same time for the next one.

Where would I find someplace to stay? The sun was already dropping behind the hills. I guessed it would soon be dark. The prospect of a night plus a whole long day in Glenmohr didn't exactly thrill me to bits.

I had ten nail-biting minutes, comparing the church clock with my watch. I could have wept. The bus had gone. I had missed it. Despair—and then the loveliest sight in the world—a tiny green bus, vintage 1960 or so, swung around into the square.

What a relief! Obviously I was in a part of the world where timetables didn't count for very much. It was evident that the bus had stopped first at the school. By the time it reached the square, the children had spread themselves and their backpacks over most of the seats.

I jumped aboard and paid my fare, and the driver got off to have a smoke. Another ten minutes passed.

He seemed surprised at my anxious questions about what time were we leaving as I leaned out of the door. He assured me we'd be leaving very soon now and going straight to Lochroy. And yes, there was a phone box in the village right where the bus stopped.

His manner, amused and rather mocking, hinted that I was a little mad being so urgent about a journey. It suggested that the word "urgent" hadn't yet been invented in this particular spot on the map. Life moved at a much slower pace than in the great city I had just left.

The children were getting noisy. There was a lot of horseplay and giggling between the boys and girls. No one was in any hurry to leave except me.

I had taken the vacant front seat behind the driver. I decided that would give me a first-class view of the landscape—if we ever got moving. Meanwhile I stared out the window at the dull little square and tried to stop biting my nails. Ahead of us lay miles of mountains, forests, streams, and some of the most beautiful scenery God had created.

I could almost hear Calum's advice. "Just relax and enjoy it. Think of the adventure with Castle Roy and its loch waiting for you." Maybe I'd even be lucky and see the monster on one of its rare appearances.

At last the driver threw away his cigarette, got on board, and started the engine. We were away!

Suddenly a now-familiar figure ran across the square. The professor!

As he got aboard, he looked back over his shoulder. He had a hunted look. It said he was being followed. He took out money for a ticket.

"Where to, sir? We just go as far as Lochroy."

"That will do."

I put out a hand as he walked past, but he didn't notice me. He looked real scared. Clutching that red leather briefcase, he staggered toward one of the rear seats. Through the driver's mirror in front of me, I watched him staring out the back window.

I was about to follow him and return the envelope and paper I'd found under his seat on the train. And his five-pound note. I'd explain about taking a long time in the dining car, missing him when we got off the train, and so forth.

However, one glance at his face told me he wouldn't be particularly interested in my tale of woe. It said that he had a lot more important things than food on his mind just then. Things that made him forget all about the burger now resting cold and soggy in my backpack.

Should I offer it to him, make the polite gesture anyway? About to leave my seat, I stopped in my tracks.

Racing toward the bus and flagging it down were the two men from the train. I knew then that my instincts had been right. They were following him and they were up to no good. He was in danger, and caution told me to keep out of it if I knew what was good for me.

But the driver, bless his heart, had no intention of stopping. Once we had left the station square, he wasn't taking on any more passengers. He swept past the two men, staring straight ahead, ignoring their frantic signals.

Everyone else on the bus saw what was happening. The children yelled and made rude faces out of the windows. The professor crouched well down in his seat, hugging that briefcase to his chest and turning his head away in an effort not to be seen.

I sighed with relief. He was safe for the moment but there was a very long, lonely journey ahead of us through deserted heath and heather with very few houses. The kind of place where anything could happen.

CHAPTER 4

The bus was old. The seats were worn, and the springs had seen better days. I soon found out that this part of the journey was going to be very slow and uncomfortable. Jolting along the road, every corner was a roller-coaster ride that had us hanging onto our seats.

The school kids didn't even notice it. But I could see the professor gazing out of the window and looking very unhappy indeed. When at last we reached a fairly straight stretch of road, I went back to give him his five-pound note.

He took it from me, stared at it blankly. I explained about the burger and the coffee, the long wait in the dining-car line. He shook his head as if he'd never seen me before.

Then at last the light seemed to dawn. "Of course, of course. I remember now. You were very kind to take so much trouble."

Realizing how little impression I made on the opposite sex, even an elderly gentleman, was not flattering. "I hoped to see you at Glenmohr, but I missed you on the station platform—"

I don't think he understood a word I was saying. He put the money in his pocket and looked more dazed than ever when I said, "You are Dr. Parker?"

He nodded. "I am."

"Then these must belong to you," I said handing him the envelope and the paper.

Before I could explain, he came suddenly to life, snatched them from me, and demanded, "Where did you get these?"

"They were under your seat in the train. You must have dropped them when you were gathering up your papers."

"Oh. That's all right, then." He calmed down suddenly and muttered, "Thank you again." Then thrusting them into his pocket, he turned his head away. Gazing out of the window, he clutched his briefcase like a newborn infant.

And that was the end of that. He closed his eyes wearily and yawned. A polite signal that he did not wish to be disturbed any further.

As I staggered back to my seat, I was disappointed. I had really been hoping he would tell me why he was on the run, why and where he had hidden on the train, how he had managed to get off at Glenmohr without being seen, and why those two men were pursuing him. Was he a spy, for instance?

All very exciting stuff and, I realized, also none of my business. Again I could just see Calum smile when I told him. "Why should he tell his whole life story to a pretty young woman just because she was thoughtful enough to offer to bring him a coffee and a burger from the dining car?" He'd laugh and kiss me. "What an imagination, Annie! Never mind, you'll grow out of it someday. It isn't a life-threatening condition."

In an old movie, of course, the professor would have looked like Cary Grant. He would have fallen for my charms and told me all. But, as I had learned, real life isn't like that.

Remembering that Calum believes I am pretty always pleases me, though. The professor had only confirmed what my looking-glass told me every day. I was a very ordinary girl with nothing to make me stand out in a crowd. A rather mousy girl with good eyes and good legs, hardly one to set the world on fire.

Only to Calum who loved me would I ever be beautiful and clever and witty. I should be content with that. Some girls never stop being Cinderella, never find their Prince Charming or the glass slipper that fits.

My seat behind the driver gave me great views of the countryside. Sitting back, I told myself that I had probably invented the whole sinister scene. The elderly man who I had decided was a professor had a name now. He was Dr Parker and he could have had a dozen reasons for leaving the train car while I was at the dining car.

He might be a sick man with an ulcer. Feeling travel-sick, he had gone to the toilet. Or he might have met someone he knew in first class and moved in to visit with them.

A dozen reasons? That was only two. And it still didn't explain why someone with an ulcer and feeling unwell would have asked for a hamburger from the dining car.

I thought about those other two men. Could they have some innocent reason for rushing up and down the train? Had I invented some sinister motive? It could be coincidence that they ran after the bus. The same bus that Dr. Parker had just caught by the skin of his teeth, so to speak. After all, it was the only bus of the day. It could be that they had business reasons for a trip to Lochroy.

Well, I wasn't ever going to find out the truth from Dr. Parker, that was for sure. So I should dismiss him from my mind and enjoy the scenery while I had the chance.

I had been told by the travel agent that this was the most romantic part of Scotland. I was entering a magic world where millions of people came from all parts of the globe to visit each year.

As we passed through the countryside, I saw regiments of fir trees, silver birches, and, everywhere, castles. Castles that were lived in and whose proud owners had flags flying from their battlements. Castles with stately terraces and smooth lawns. Castles that Snow White might have loved, dark and full of mystery.

Then there were the ruins of castles, belonging to Scotland's history, with only one wall still standing. I had never seen so many castles. It seemed that everyone in this stretch of the Highlands lived in one.

The only other buildings were small farms perched high in the hills and roofless cottages. Sad homes abandoned more than a century ago when the landlords cleared the land and replaced their tenants with more profitable sheep. Those same tenants fled to America and Australia to begin new lives, taking only their names to remind them of a bitter past.

There was a lot of hilarity on the bus. The school kids called out to the driver, Jock, and shouted teasing remarks at him. He knew them all by name, took their taunts, and gave as good as he got from them. Just as well the road was empty, I thought, as they diverted his attention. There were few passing places as we climbed the steep hillside.

But I had spoken too soon.

Suddenly Jock swore. Looking through his mirror I saw the reason. A car, a white Ford, had crept up behind us and was trying to pass us on the narrow road.

Jock hit the horn. "Damn fool! He'll have us all into the ditch if he isn't careful."

I asked if there was a passing place ahead. "Yes. On the other side of this hill. There's a straight stretch of road once we get down to the loch. I'll try and let him through then."

The car was weaving back and forth behind us, far too close for safety.

"Have you ever seen anything like that? A school bus too! You'd think he'd show some goddamned sense."

Far below as we sped downhill I saw a gleaming of water. Beyond it, on the other side of the loch, lay a gray huddle of houses, a village of sorts.

The kids, far from being scared, were enjoying the chase. They were making rude faces at the car driver, shouting smart remarks, as kids will. I turned around to see how the professor was taking it.

He stared straight ahead, gray-faced and mighty scared-looking.

"There's Loch Roy, over there," shouted the driver to me. "Looks near enough to wade across, doesn't it? But we have to go right around it. Oh, dammit—"

He swerved the wheel violently as the car shot past us. We heard the scrape of metal on metal. The rude shouts from the school kids became screams of terror as we were hurled from our seats.

We were almost in the ditch. Jock tried desperately to get the bus back onto the road. The white Ford was in front of us now. A moment's hesitation and then it was off again at high speed down the road.

"He nearly had us all killed!" one of the girls shrieked.

"I'm going to tell my dad," said another. "He'll have him put in jail."

There was a hush among the kids at that, as if they knew all about her dad. He obviously was a man of some importance.

I scribbled down the registration number before the car disappeared from sight. There were two people inside. Two men, I thought.

But we were in trouble. The bus, old and infirm at the best of times, now clanked and stuttered. Its engine choked and spluttered as we continued down the road. I looked back and felt rather sick.

Another yard and we would have all been down the steep bank and into the loch. I was curious to see how Dr. Parker was taking this little drama. One glance was enough to tell me that he was a very unhappy man.

Was it possible that the two in the car could have been the same men who had been searching for him on the train?

Of course, that wasn't possible. Although we were traveling very slowly at no more than about thirty miles per hour on difficult roads, they had no transportation when we had left Glenmohr. I had seen them miss the bus. It takes a little time to hire a car in big towns, and Glenmohr didn't look like the kind of place where cars could be rented.

Unless they were crooks and had stolen a car! I felt pleased with myself that I'd made a note of the registration number. That would be useful in tracking them down.

Meanwhile, the bus limped along. The clanking grew louder and Jock said, "The next village is Corriedon about four miles down the road. I'll do my best to get you there. We might just make it, but I think we're losing oil. And by the sound of it, the exhaust pipe is damaged. You kids back there," he shouted, "are you all for Corriedon?"

"Ye-ss, Jock!" was the shout.

"Aren't some of you for Lochroy?"

"Angus and Billy are off school with mumps!"

The driver nodded. "Just as well. I'd clean forgotten that they weren't with me this morning." He turned to me. "I'm sorry, miss, but I wouldn't count on this bus getting you to Lochroy tonight."

"That's okay. If there's a phone, I can ring Castle Roy—that's where I'm heading. I'm sure they'll come and collect me. And drop off the gentleman at the back to wherever he's going."

Jock looked through his mirror to the still figure of Dr. Parker clutching his briefcase and nodded. "Problem solved then."

Ten minutes later we limped into Corrledon with a great deal of noise and clouds of smoke pouring from the engine.

The kids leaped off, most of them complaining that they lived on farms two miles away and Jock usually put them off at the end of their roads.

He grinned. "A couple of miles won't harm you to walk for once. It's a fine day for it. Just be thankful it isn't raining," he added, kicking at one of the wheels as if it had personally offended him. But the action was good-natured, I thought. The way you'd treat a difficult but well-loved animal.

When he saw me watching him, he said, "I don't like being defeated. I'm a whiz kid with old cars; you have to be in my job. I might just get it to hang together till I get home, but I wouldn't care to risk passengers."

He pointed to the phone box. "Over there, miss. You'll manage, will you? You can fill in time and get a cup of tea while you wait. It should only take them twenty minutes from the castle."

When I said how sorry I was that he'd landed in all

this trouble, he grinned. "It's not the first time the old bus has broken down. Nor the last, I reckon. But folks are always willing to help out. It has to be like that when you live miles away from towns."

To Dr. Parker who had got off behind me and was listening, Jock said, "And you, sir. The young lady here is arranging a lift from Lochroy. I'm sure they'll drop you off wherever you want to go."

Dr. Parker frowned and looked vague. He didn't seem very grateful for the offer.

"How will you get home?" I said to Jock.

Again he smiled. "The wife's cousin owns the gas pump here. He keeps a bicycle parked behind the teashop. I'll go home on that if I can't get my string-and-glue job to work on the bus."

He looked over at the professor. "You'll be all right, sir?"

Dr. Parker stared at us, nodded, and began walking quickly toward the loch as if he had some purpose in mind.

The school kids disappeared down the road and I was left to explore Corriedon. It seemed to consist of a gas pump beside a wooden shed and a phone box. The wooden shed had a few old ads for cornflakes and baked beans in the window. There were also some very faded postcards and a hand-painted sign saying "Teas."

At that moment it was the most welcoming sight in the whole world.

But first I must phone the castle and tell them what had happened.

I dialed the number. It gave a few rings and then switched to the answering machine. "You have reached Castle Roy . . ." I listened and left my message as requested.

The teashop was empty. I had expected to see the professor seated at one of the four tiny tables. They had

bright plastic cloths and vases of bright plastic flowers.
Someone had gone to considerable effort to interest the
few tourists who came by.

A very old lady almost bent double hobbled toward me.
"Tea, is it? And would you be wanting a scone with it?"

I said yes and the result was a pot of really good, strong
tea and two large, delicious scones, piping hot out of the
oven. They came thick with jam and heavy with cream.

Feeling human again at last, I had just emerged from
the door marked Toilets. There were three steps up to a
throne-like seat and a flush worked by a heavy brass
chain. A regal lavatory that would have found favor with
good old Queen Victoria herself!

Another cup of tea? Why not. I was just lifting it to
my lips when I heard the sound of a car engine and the
unmistakable clanking of the school bus.

I seized my backpack, put down a couple of pounds for
the tea, and rushed out. I looked around for Dr. Parker.
He was nowhere to be seen, but he must have heard the
noise of the engine. Corriedon wasn't big enough to get
lost in. No doubt he would appear in a moment.

I was glad Jock had managed to get the bus started
after all. I had a very nasty feeling about waiting here and
taking a chance that my phone message had been
received. I am always uneasy about talking to machines.
As I ran along the road, I knew that if the car from
Castle Roy was on its way already, we would meet it
along the way and Jock could flag it down.

"Wait!" I shouted and raced after the slowly moving bus.

CHAPTER
5

Jock seemed surprised to see me there, banging on the bus door. He switched off the engine and when I tried to jump aboard, he said, "Just testing, miss."

"Great! That's fine by me."

He shook his head. "I doubt if we'll get as far as Lochroy."

"I'll chance it," I said firmly.

"No. I'm sorry, miss. I can't take you. These aren't the sort of roads to take risks on. You don't want to end up in the loch." Being left in Corriedon didn't seem like the kind of choice I'd like to make, either. Jock continued, "I can't take the risk of injury to a passenger."

He let that sink in before adding, "I saw you phoning. Just you play safe, miss. Wait for your lift. They'll be here soon," he added hopefully.

Perhaps he was right. Anyway, I knew he had no

intention of letting me risk life and limb. The bus was
empty except for a bike perched between two seats
behind him.

He saw me looking at it and grinned. "That's for
emergencies. That's how sure I feel about reaching
Lochroy this night."

I looked back along the road. There was still no sign
of Dr. Parker, who must have heard the sound of the bus
by now.

"What about the other passenger?" I asked.

"What other passenger would that be, miss?" Jock
frowned, his mind elsewhere. Clearly Dr. Parker hadn't
made much impression on him.

"The man you stopped and picked up as we left the
square in Glenmohr," I explained.

"Oh, the old gentleman, you mean. Well, the castle
folk will drop him off when they come to collect you."

"I don't know where he's gone," I said. "I haven't seen
him since we arrived here, have you?"

"No," said Jock, sounding puzzled by the question.
I could sympathize with that. He had troubles enough
with a broken-down bus without accounting for Dr.
Parker's taking off somewhere.

"We told him about the car coming from the castle for
you, miss. It's up to him whether he wants a lift or not.
Maybe he decided to walk." And he started up the engine.

I stepped back on the road and stood there watching
the bus clanking down the long road beside the tree-lined
loch. He had hardly traveled more than a hundred yards
when there was a loud bang, then a cloud of blue smoke
followed by silence.

I was already running toward it in case Jock was
injured when he emerged from the bus. Dragging out

that bicycle and mounting it, he vanished around a bend in the road without even looking back.

There was nothing to do but wait for the Stuarts' car. My refuge, the teashop, now had a "Closed" sign on the door. It looked like Corriedon only came to life twice a day when the school bus passed through.

As for other vehicles, there was not so much as a parked car anywhere. Not even a television antenna. It didn't look as if Corriedon had much contact with the world beyond the waters of the loch. I doubted whether, surrounded by high mountains, they would ever get a TV picture clear enough to be worth watching anyway.

Well, I should be grateful for that one link with civilization, the phone that would get me out of here as soon as possible.

I dialed Castle Roy. Once again I got the answering machine. I slammed down the receiver. There is nothing more maddening in this world than a recorded message when you need urgently to speak to a real live person.

I looked at my watch. Without all these delays over the breakdown, the bus would have been in Lochroy by now. The Stuarts were probably waiting, wondering what had happened to me. I sat down at the roadside and thought about what to do next. Sitting waiting didn't appeal in the least, and the sensible thing seemed to be to start walking.

I tried to picture the scene on the other side of the loch. Jock on his bicycle would tell the Stuarts that he had left me in Corriedon. Surely then they would guess that I was heading toward them on foot.

I hoped so anyway. At least, I told myself, that is how I would have behaved.

I took one last look around the deserted village. Before leaving I must find out what had become of Dr. Parker.

The fact that he hadn't come back when he heard the bus worried me. When he got on at Glenmohr, he had paid his fare to Lochroy. That must have been his destination too. I remembered him nodding vaguely when Jock said the castle car would drop him off when they came to collect me.

Where had he gone after he disappeared through the trees down to the lochside? The village of Corriedon was one long street huddled at the bottom of a steep mountain road. The road most likely led to a farm on the hillside somewhere.

That could hardly have been where Dr. Parker was heading. The bus breaking down at Corriedon was as much a surprise to him as it was to me. The scared way he reacted suggested that all he wanted was to dodge his pursuers. Where the bus was going at that moment didn't concern him as long as it provided a means of escape.

He seemed so frightened sitting at the back of the bus, staring out of the window. The more I thought about it, the less I liked just walking away. For one thing, he didn't look equipped to go marching off about the countryside with only a briefcase.

Come to think of it, what had happened to the rest of the luggage he must have had when he left London? The rack above our seats on the train had been empty. And he certainly had no extra baggage when he boarded the bus in Glenmohr.

Dr. Parker was elderly, a bit vague, and none too fit, I thought. Haunted by Dad's recent accident, I knew how easy it could be for Dr. Parker to fall and break a limb. My conscience, to say nothing of my curiosity, would not allow me to continue my journey. I couldn't abandon the professor without knowing why he hadn't appeared again when Jock got the bus started.

I had to make sure that he wasn't lying injured without anyone to help him.

It didn't take long to scramble down to the lochside. There was Lochroy shimmering across the water. It looked so close. I sighed deeply, thinking of the miles of twisting roads that separated me from that village.

I stood on a pebbled shore all alone with only a rowboat moored at the water's edge. In the center of the loch was a tiny island with an ancient ruin. The remains of yet another slice of Scottish history, a castle with broken walls and windows.

I shouted, "Hello there?" My voice sounded very loud and I felt foolish when there was no response. Not that I honestly expected the professor to reply. I knew I had better give up searching for him, climb back to the roadside, and start walking.

At that moment my foot crunched on glass. A broken bottle, I thought, left by some hiker. I looked again.

A pair of glasses with horn rims and thick lenses.

I had a cold feeling of dismay as I held them in my hand. These I was sure were the ones Dr. Parker had been wearing. Like all shortsighted people, he would never willingly be parted from his glasses since he wouldn't be able to see a thing without them.

As I stood wondering what to do next, I heard the most beautiful sound in the world—a car was coming down the road.

Castle Roy to the rescue!

I leaped up the bank and waved frantically. Then I recognized the car. A white Ford, the same one that had forced the bus off the road. The same car that had almost put us all in the loch.

But beggars cannot be choosers. So I decided to take

my life in my hands and persuade the reckless driver to take me to Lochroy.

I was near enough now to recognize that there were two men in the car. The driver and his passenger were the same two men from the train who had tried to get onto the bus.

They were alone and the backseat was empty. How they had found a car so quickly didn't concern me at that moment. As they slowed down, I was suddenly more scared than I had ever been in my life.

I was alone on a deserted road. I could scream for help and no one would hear me. But there was no way on earth I would go willingly into that car with them.

Even as I quickly turned away, they spotted me and stopped. The young guy leaped out

"Wait, miss. Wait. Hold on."

I decided to play it cool, bluff my way out. "Yes? What is it?"

He grinned. "Well, well. The hitchhiker. You were on the bus, miss. We saw you on the train too. You were traveling with Dr. Parker, weren't you?"

So they knew who he was. But before I could deny it, the other man cursed his partner, breathed a warning too late.

I shook my head and tried to look confused. He went on, "Problems with your transportation, miss? Can we offer you a lift to wherever you're heading?"

They knew the bus had broken down because it was their fault. I was suddenly not only scared but angry.

"Come along, miss. You come with us. We'll take you to Lochroy," said the young guy, putting a hand on my arm.

I looked at his hand as if it were some particularly horrible reptile. "No, thank you. I prefer to walk."

"It's nearly six miles."

"So what? I like walking."

"I really think this time you should come with us," said the older man, beginning to sound impatient.

"Yes, we'd really like your company. We want to have you ride with us for a while," leered the young guy.

The way he looked me over would have made Calum knock him down. What he had in mind, at least, was unmistakable.

"Please leave me alone." No longer able to deal with the situation, I panicked. I backed away.

He grabbed my arm firmly now. "Don't take on like that, miss. There's nothing to be scared about. We're all grownups—"

"Let me go!" I yelled despite the fact that no one could hear me.

As I struggled, his grip tightened. With one hand he opened the passenger door and tried to thrust me inside. I took advantage of his being slightly off balance and kicked out, very hard.

He cried out, swore, and let me go. Before the older man could get out of the car, I was away like the wind, sprinting toward the lochside. The way Dr. Parker had gone, never to return. But there were trees and vegetation, somewhere to hide.

I was too scared to think straight beyond running for dear life. My backpack caught on a branch. I stumbled, fell heavily, and slithered down toward some bushes. I dived into them and crouched low, lying still, hardly breathing.

Above me I heard the sound of branches breaking and then I heard their voices close at hand. I was sure they could hear my heart beating, it was so loud. There were more sounds of swishing branches over my head which seemed to last for ever. Then silence. I lay still. I guessed they were listening too for any movements.

"Let's go," said the older man. He sounded weary. "We've seen enough of this damned part of the loch today."

"She can't be far away." A laugh. "I kinda liked her. My type—"

"I know your type. Let's go," the older man repeated.

Some footsteps. "Okay. What if she finds out . . . ?" The last words were lost.

A coarse laugh. "Small chance of that . . . " He added something more which they both found very amusing. Their footsteps retreated and at last I heard the sound of a car engine.

I waited, shivering, until I was absolutely sure they had driven away before I came out of hiding. I guessed something awful had happened to the professor and that the pair of spectacles I had found had been dropped by him. I imagined him running, hunted down by his pursuers.

I shivered. Whatever the young guy was thinking about, I doubted whether it would have included a happy ending. I couldn't see myself arriving safely, my backpack intact at the door of Castle Roy.

At last I decided it was safe to come out of the bushes. But when I tried to walk, I realized that something awful had happened—it was agony! When I had slid into the bushes, my ankle had twisted painfully under me. I had been too concerned about hiding from the two men to pay much attention then. Thank heaven it wasn't broken, just a bad sprain, I thought—boots had saved a worse injury.

But when I put my weight on it, I groaned. There was no way I was going to walk one mile, let alone six. I limped to the roadside and sat down again, nursing my ankle.

What on earth would I do if the car from Castle Roy didn't arrive?

There was a sunset on the loch. The clouds looked like the entrance to another, better world—a sight I would have marveled at in happier times. But all it meant to me now was the danger I was in. Once the glorious crimson light on the water faded, it would be completely dark.

As dark as it never is in towns where there are streetlamps. Pitch dark—dark where you can't see a hand before your face. Dark where the only light is from stars billions of miles away and not much use at all for seeing the road before you.

It was getting colder too, and huddled on the bank with an aching ankle, I guessed that there had been a change of plan. There was no car coming for me this night.

Answering machines, as I knew even in Edinburgh, were not always reliable.

Well, I didn't want to sit in Corriedon until morning. A wooden shed well padlocked and a gas pump didn't offer much shelter for a cozy night's sleep.

Of course, there might be a farm up that road. Or the road in the direction the white Ford had taken. But I doubted whether I'd be able to limp that far in any case.

And then I remembered. On the pebbled shore of the lochside, just a few yards along from where I had found the professor's broken glasses, I had seen a boat moored.

A rowboat.

CHAPTER 6

I hobbled around but there were no signs of leaks in the boat. It looked seaworthy enough.

Time will tell, I thought grimly, *once I get it afloat. If it has holes below the waterline and begins to sink, I can always swim back to shore again*, I told myself cheerfully. But I was really very scared at leaving dry land.

Should I climb up the bank and try the phone once more before setting off? Surely the Stuarts would be back at Castle Roy by now. Across the water the hillside above Lochroy village was dotted with lights. People in those remote farms and houses were settling down for the evening. What bliss, to be safe in a warm kitchen with food on the table!

I stumbled on a heavy stick as I tried to decide what to do. I picked it up, grateful for a cane to lean on. Faintly I heard the hum of a car engine. Sounds carry a long way

across water, and these were not coming from the direction
of Lochroy. They came from the wrong side of Corriedon.

And that made me think twice about the effort
involved in stumbling back up to the road. What if the
two men were back again? In my present state I was
helpless to run away from them.

I inspected the boat and its two oars. They looked sturdy
enough. I'd take a chance on it. Come to think of it, I hadn't
any other option. So I tore a page out of my notebook and
scribbled a note which I anchored under a stone.

"Sorry—I had to borrow your boat and will pay you
for the use of it. Please phone Castle Roy and ask for
Annie Kelty. Will explain all then."

It wasn't as hard as I had thought to slip off the chain
and step into the boat. Although my boots got wet on
the outside, they were waterproof, and the icy water on
my sore ankle was sheer bliss.

Once aboard, I sat for a moment testing the oars and
getting the feel of them. I was bobbing about with the
slight current but the boat seemed to be watertight.
Taking a deep breath, I used one oar to push against a big
rock near the shore.

At the first push, I thought it wasn't going to work.
I was afraid I'd have to get out and push the boat clear
of the shore using my own feeble strength.

Then, suddenly, there was a scraping sound and the
boat was on the wet sand that sloped steeply into the
loch. With a final wobble it moved clear of land and hit
the water.

I grabbed the oars and held them firmly against the
current. To my surprise it wasn't as hard to row as I had
thought. With very little effort on my part, I was soon
drifting several yards away from the shore, and I realized

that the current was in my favor. It would take me in the right direction, straight over to Loch Roy.

Looking back toward Corriedon, I gave a sigh of relief. At least I was safe here from Dr. Parker's pursuers, and for the first time I began to enjoy this part of the adventure. Wait until I told Calum. To be honest, I didn't know much about rowboats. My one and only experience was a school holiday spent with one of my friends in the Lake District.

Her father had a fishing boat on Lake Windermere, and her elder brother used to take us out and let us do the rowing. He liked to lie there reading and shouting orders to us, letting us do the hard work. I always remembered that holiday. I got a taste for rowing.

But that was ten years ago.

You've always wanted to try it again, Annie, I told myself. *Now's your big chance.*

The last rays of sunset had now fled from the loch. The waves were no longer golden but a very pale, cold-looking blue. The moon I had seen earlier was hidden by heavy clouds. In other circumstances and with Calum, the man I loved, at my side, I would have thought it was all very beautiful and romantic.

But to be practical, as I knew I had to be to survive on my own, I hoped we weren't in for a storm. A flight of starlings roosting on the tiny island were disturbed by some unseen danger. They took off into the sky in a screeching, noisy cloud.

A moment later in the silence, I noticed a jet-stream across the sky from some outward-bound plane. A reminder of the busy world I had left just a few short hours ago, a time that seemed to belong on another planet.

I was starting to get the hang of rowing again. The oars

dipping into the water, the creak of the boat were the only sounds. I shipped the oars for a moment and let the current take over.

Bliss! And as I suspected, we were heading gently in the direction of the far shore and Lochroy village. The moon came riding out from behind the clouds. Magic! I breathed in the air. So clear and cold, sharp as a glass of chilled wine.

Then, when I least expected it, there was a scraping sound under the boat and it wobbled dangerously. Had I hit a submerged rock? Panic! I looked over the side, hanging on like grim death. Something very large hit the bottom of the boat. For a fraction of a moment, it moved alongside. A big black shape distorted by the water.

The shadows were too dark to see clearly but it looked—

It looked like a body floating, face downward, arms outstretched . . .

The missing Dr. Parker, I thought. *God, how horrible!*

But the boat needed all my efforts to keep on course. It rocked violently and we were going to capsize. I balanced fearfully, holding on to the sides. What would I do if I found myself in the loch beside the body of a drowned man?

There was a sudden stirring alongside the boat now— I hadn't time to see if it was Dr. Parker. That big black shape just under the surface moved again.

IT WAS ALIVE—

THE MONSTER IN THE LOCH—

And I was about to meet the fate that befell people in boats on Loch Roy. People who disappeared never to be seen again. I thought about screaming to scare it away, or would it be safer to lie low, so that it thought the boat was empty?

As the boat continued to rock dangerously, I knew I must hang on at all costs. I mustn't fall into the water. That would be playing into its claws or jaws—whatever monsters use to grind up their prey.

I wasn't giving in without a fight, and I poised one oar ready to strike. I waited. Nothing happened, but the boat was still again. Had it gone? And then I saw it, a few feet away: a sleek black head and neck arose above the water. A glimpse of eyes, a jaw, a tongue.

"Go away!" I screamed. "Go away!"

I couldn't reach it but I hit out at the water with the oar, hoping that would scare it off. There was a hideous noise like a growl or a roar, and the next moment it submerged.

I sat back, my heart beating wildly. I listened. Nothing but the silence of the night came back to me.

Turning to pick up the second oar and set off again, I saw only an empty lock. In my panic, I had let the oar fall into the water. I looked around frantically.

Damn—oh damn! As if on cue, the clouds I had thought of as part of a romantic sunset turned into sheets of rain.

I was suddenly terrified. I was alone on a loch with a monster and no human being within earshot. No one on this earth could help me.

I tried desperately to think what to do next, aware that my life depended on getting across to Lochroy before the storm broke. I began to use my one oar with great vigor. I was crying now, scared, so scared. "Help me, oh please God, help me!" My tears mingled with the sleety rain.

It was bitterly cold but in no time I was sweating with exertion, thankful that my hooded jacket was rainproof.

Whatever happened, I was going to get very wet, and although I had stopped crying, I could no longer see anything across the water. With my head down and my back toward Lochroy, I rowed and rowed. I had lost all count of time or aching shoulders when at last my efforts were rewarded by the most beautiful sight in the whole world: land! In record time I had reached the other side of the loch. I was safe at last.

Only when I blinked the rain off my face, I saw it wasn't Lochroy village after all. My vigorous rowing with only one oar had washed the boat up to the tiny island in the middle of the loch.

I don't often give in, but I put my head down and howled with misery and pain.

Of course, that didn't help any more than my tears of fright. Crying was just a waste of time and a drain on the energy I needed. So I dried my eyes and pushed back my hood. I must be practical and find a way out of this disaster.

The sleet had turned into a fine drizzle. That was something. Perhaps my prayers had been answered, so I stopped feeling sorry for myself. I was shivering but not with fear. Now that my exertion of fast rowing was over, the cold settled on me like a shroud. Even my jacket wasn't much protection for someone sitting still in the middle of a loch in this kind of weather.

It would be dark soon, but there were areas of light on the fringes of the clouds as if the moon were struggling to put in another appearance. After the freezing temperature of the storm, the sudden change had left a fine vapor of mist swirling a few feet above the water.

At any other time, it would have looked very pretty indeed. Now I shuddered. I could see it only as an added danger. Mist would provide the perfect conditions for a monster on the loose.

I hoped Dr. Parker was not a floating corpse, but there was no way I was going to risk going back to find out for sure.

I considered my options. With only one oar, I might never reach Lochroy and safety before the monster had another shot at upsetting the boat and grabbing me.

The only alternative was this tiny island and the ruined castle I had seen from Corriedon. The castle was invisible from where I sat, but surely it would offer some kind of shelter.

The good news was that there would be sticks and wood to make a fire—just like they did in old movies. The bad news was that since I don't smoke, I have no reason to carry matches. So I wasn't likely to have much success in that direction.

Whatever happened, it promised to be a night to remember, the longest and scariest in my whole life.

CHAPTER 7

Soon it had stopped raining, the storm clouds replaced by a clear sky. A typical Highland weather change: sudden and dangerous. Now as the boat neared the island, moonlight turned night into day and the loch was a gleaming expanse of silver.

Preparing to set foot on the pebbled shore, I was suddenly afraid. Although all was silent around me, I thought about the monster again. Had it been some floating object, the log of a tree? I shuddered at that first impression of a corpse floating face downward, arms outstretched.

The missing Dr. Parker.

Knowing that what I had mistaken for arms were most probably the beast's flippers wasn't a great deal of comfort. Not if what I saw emerging from the water—the head, long neck, ferocious eyes, and mouth—were those of the monster of Loch Roy.

Or was that a trick of my imagination, my fears? The

branches of a floating tree by moonlight? I sat in the
boat, reluctant to move and suddenly homesick as I had
never been in my life before. The thought of Edinburgh
made me want to weep.

My passion for adventure had died, killed stone dead
this night. What I wouldn't have given to wake up in the
morning in my safe, warm bed and find that the past few
hours were part of some dreadful nightmare. At home, of
course, I would laugh like everyone else. How could
anyone believe in monsters in lochs in this day and age?
Such legends were for the tourist trade. Something to
scare little children in the days before television made
them immune to horrors.

I crawled out of the boat but could find nothing firm
enough to fix the chain around. The pier had rotted long
ago, so with considerable effort I dragged the boat onto
the pebbled shore. And there I left it.

In saner moments without so many problems about losing
buses and being pursued by a couple of crooks and having a
sprained ankle, I would have given more careful thought to
the business of making sure that boat was securely anchored.
But my main concern—all I could think about—was being
tired and hungry. I was cold but fortunately my jacket had
saved me from getting soaked through.

However, all the signs were that things weren't going
to get better. I'd stay cold until morning when I would be
rescued. I was assuming, of course, that people from the
village across the water going about their daily business
sometimes paused to glance in the direction of the island
to admire its ruined castle.

If my frantic signals and shouts were ignored, then I
still had another chance. I would row across to Lochroy.
With one oar and very slow progress, I could still make it.
But to try at night with monsters around was something I
preferred not to think about.

What still bothered me was why the Stuarts hadn't made more effort to find out what had happened to me after the bus broke down. They must have heard about it by now even if the answering machine wasn't working.

Thinking more calmly, I tried to make excuses for them. According to Dad, they ran the castle as a luxury hotel. Most likely on a shoestring budget, they did the cooking themselves with few servants. When there were guests, they might well have a very strict schedule about meals to prepare—a schedule that would have fitted neatly into a plan to meet me in the late afternoon but would have been impossible later.

Stumbling up the steep incline to the castle, the moonlight revealed that it was worse than I had expected. There were stinging nettles everywhere. I had to beat a path through them with the stick that I needed to help me walk.

At last I stood beneath the tall, forbidding ruin of the castle. I could now see plainly, however, that there was more to the ruin than I had first seen as only one wall.

The moon shone on the remains of a once fine arched door. After a few hearty shoves with my shoulder, it gave way. The creaking of the ancient door disturbed a whole army of small animals and rodents, sending them scurrying to the safety of their holes. I closed my eyes, trying not to think of spiders beneath my feet and bats above my head.

A dark cloud of rooks rose into the sky. Their screams of rage were the last thing my shattered nerves needed just then. I was really scared and, taking a deep breath, I waited for silence again. I would walk carefully, hoping not to meet any of the castle's present four-footed or winged-and-clawed residents.

After the last faint squeak and rustle, I went inside.

Guided by the moonlight, I picked my way across fallen
stones, broken floors, and walls whose only decoration
was now bird droppings. The occasional crash of stones
or rotten timber that I had disturbed had my scalp
crawling with terror.

Nothing would have surprised me in that eerie setting.
No ghost rattling chains could have scared me any more
than the natural horrors and decay all around me. As in
most Scottish castles built for defense, the only entrance
was by a narrow, clockwise, spiral staircase.

This left the defender's sword arm free. The grim idea
was that your enemies would be fighting their way
upwards. They could be picked off and cut down one at a
time as you forced them downward to ground level.

As I climbed past narrow slit-like windows, (not to let
light in but to fire arrows out at the enemy), the steps
that remained were broken and crumbling. Dad's
accident had happened on our perfectly well-restored
spiral stair, which had got me into all this awful mess. So
I took my time, walking very slowly and carefully.

Pausing to give my sore ankle a rest, I looked through
one of the slits across the loch to the floodlit turrets of
Castle Roy. I was filled with envy for this grand, brave
sight. And for those visitors whose only thoughts were on
excellent food and wine and a comfortable bed after a
warm and deeply scented bath.

Away from the moonlight, the air was suddenly icy on
my face and I stopped just in time. The staircase had ended
abruptly, and I was standing above thin air with only the
sky and its stars between me and the ground far below.

As I stepped back hastily, there was another warning
rumble of falling stones. I felt my way along the opposite
wall and touched a stone doorway.

The moon shone into a room with an arched window,

fragments of floor, and an enormous fireplace. Beyond there was nothing but space and the ghostly, waving branches of tall trees. Only a massive pile of stones, plaster, and wood at ground level remained of the other half of what had once been the castle's pride and joy, the Great Hall.

I looked around me, stricken by the forlorn sight. Was it only the wind sighing through the great empty window? I seemed to hear the swish of silk and to feel breath on my face. The once still air seemed full of whispering voices, as if all the people who had lived and died here had gathered and were trying to tell me something. If only I could understand the words, hear what they were saying through the thick gray veil of time.

I knew that something very strange had happened to me, something for which I could find no explanation. From the moment I had stood in Corriedon and looked across at the tiny island in the middle of the loch with the rowing boat on the shore below me, I had a feeling that I'd been here before. A feeling that all this was part of a lost pattern in my life, like the replay of a film made long ago.

Had I once before stood on a pebbled beach and watched a rowboat? But there the scene cut off. There was no more, only darkness. No more memories.

What was that? Alarmed, I jumped as yet another stone loosened by my climb whistled down past the window and thudded onto the ground far below. It scared the birds who had grumpily retired for the night.

Above my head, into the open sky they soared, screaming, great black ragged shapes fluttering across the loch. Other birds joined in the chorus of panic, and the air echoed with cries—sad, desolate, lost.

I was on a broken stairway going nowhere, alone in an unsafe ruin where I could lie injured for days. Where I could die and perhaps never be found until years later.

At that nasty thought, I made my way down to ground level as fast as I could go. As I fled, I saw to my left what I had failed to notice on the upward climb. Up three steps there was another broken door, hanging by its hinges.

I squeezed around it and found myself in a once handsome room. All that remained were stained walls with bird droppings, a huge fireplace, and two empty windows staring down on the loch with weeds growing through their stone sills.

The monstrous shape of a broken four-poster bed with a canopy loomed across the floor. As I staggered over, loose and rotted floorboards leaped into the air. However, it was not the bed that interested me, only its heavy velvet curtains.

Although they were ancient and thick with dust, here was something to wrap myself in until morning came, to keep me from freezing to death. There were some broken chairs, and there was even a "garde-robe," the earliest known toilet in the world—straight over the loch!

I tugged at the curtains which were so rotted they came away from the bed in my hands. Dragging them across the floor, I wrapped them around me and sat on the windowsill where I could keep an eye on any movement on the far side of the loch.

Now that I felt reasonably safe for a little while, I opened my backpack. I had troubles enough for the moment. The wooden box would have to wait until morning when I would soon discover whether the precious goblet had been damaged during this nightmare trip from Edinburgh.

Hunger was all I could think about. And there was the hamburger I had brought from the dining car on the train for the professor—cold now and the bun rather soggy. It was still the best possible burger in the whole world.

Never had any food tasted as good as this. And the Coke and chocolate bar Susie had given me for the journey. God bless her!

As I ate, I longed only to be warm. If only I could light a fire, I could rest content until morning. I did feel better once I took off my damp socks and put on dry ones. But oddly enough after all my day's grim adventures, I didn't feel at all sleepy. Perhaps it was that four-poster bed across the floor haunted by the ghosts of past generations that made me nervous. How many men and women through the ages, young and old, happy or sad, had breathed their last in its depths?

Having eaten, I was beginning to feel uneasy about the rowboat, which I couldn't see from the window. Before I settled for the night, I should make sure that it was securely tied on the beach. Beside the bed was a strong cord that had seen better days as a bell pull to summon the servants. It was just what I needed and I staggered down those uneven steps once more. Much to my surprise my ankle seemed less painful, just a mild sprain after all.

Outside the moonlight was brighter than ever. "Thank you, God, for a moon," I said as I made my way carefully back to the pebbled beach.

I blinked. There was no boat. . . .

For a moment I thought I had been mistaken, that I was on the wrong side of the island. No, this was the path I'd made, there were the broken nettles leading up to the castle.

And I had made no mistake. There was my boat, twenty yards away, a tiny black shape bobbing its way across the water toward Lochroy.

I tried not to give way and scream. I was truly stranded. Even with one oar, I could have managed somehow if no one came to rescue me in the morning.

For tonight at least I had shelter, a place to sleep. I must keep calm. To keep company with my gloomy thoughts, a heavy cloud drifted across the moon. It was pitch black for a moment, and I shivered in a bitter wind suddenly stirring across the hills, the kind of wind that brings snow from the north.

All around me was silence, a world deep in sleep. I could yell for help forever but who would hear me in Lochroy even if my voice carried all that way? So feeling very depressed indeed, I made my way back up the spiral staircase to what I hoped again was not the most haunted room in the castle.

A final look out of the window. There was nothing between me and Lochroy but this island and the loch. The floodlights had been switched off at Castle Roy. There was total darkness. I guessed that with little to entertain them in the evenings, the folks hereabouts went to bed early.

And so wrapping myself in one of the curtains, which had me choking in clouds of dust, I prepared to settle down for the night. The curtain smelled of mold, damp, and decay but it was thick enough to keep out the cold until daylight.

I closed my eyes, determined to rest, but images of the day and its disasters drifted through my mind. I sighed wearily and told myself to be thankful for small things like shelter for the night and a smelly curtain to wrap myself in. But even if I were lucky enough to drift off to sleep, would I be safe? What dreams and discomforts, what nightmares lay in wait?

After half an hour I gave up. Something outside alerted me. Had I dreamed that sound from the loch?

I ran to the window and shouted, "Hello—hello!"

Perhaps they couldn't hear me and were on the other

side of the island. Someone was certainly out there. I was about to be rescued. The empty boat had drifted ashore. The Stuarts had realized what had happened—

I listened again. The sound on the water was a splashing, gentle and regular, the sound that oars would make although it was too dark to see the boat.

I waited no longer. Unwrapping the curtain, I went down the spiral staircase as quickly as I could. On the pebbled shore, the mist swirled. It was too dark to see anything clearly.

"Hello!" I called. "Hello—I'm over here!"

I waited. There was no answer. But there was no break in the paddling sounds either, that familiar splashing of water made by oars—or a swimmer close at hand.

Why was there no reply? For a moment I panicked. Then I knew that my reasoning had been all wrong. Of course, there must be some current on the water. The rowboat I had lost was drifting back to the island. I scrambled along the pebbled shore, following the sound.

Then, like a curtain being raised, the moon came from behind the clouds and shone like a searchlight on the water.

About twenty feet away, a dark shape moved on the edge of the mist, chopping at the surface of the still water.

But it was no boat.

BOATS DON'T BREATHE. . . .

What I saw was alive. Its shape in the water wasn't very clear. But it was very large and very dark. It had a head, a neck, eyes, and a mouth. And it was swimming toward the shore—toward me.

It was the same creature I had seen earlier on the loch. It had tried to overturn my boat, and it had followed me to the island. Now I was at its mercy with no place to hide. I screamed. I clawed my way back up the bank through the nettles. Once inside the door, I leaned against it and forced it closed.

I listened, trying to hear what was outside against the noise of my own breathing. Suddenly I heard a sound that turned my heart to stone: a scrabbling on the pebbled shore I had just left, a rattling sound of one stone against another.

As if that Something walked.

Without moonlight now, I edged my way toward the staircase. In a timeless eternity of fear, on hands and knees, I groped my way up the broken steps. Sobbing, I prayed that monsters didn't know how to open doors and climb spiral stairs.

"Run! Run!" my screaming nerves shouted. My ankle was hurting again with the extra exertion and dragging me back down. At last I reached the bedroom and ran to the window overlooking the loch.

Far below, mist crawled in phantom shapes above the water. It was a scene out of a horror film.

CHAPTER
8

After a while, I decided
that I was safe in my window above the treetops on the
island. Safe, that is, from everything now except my own
imagination. So taking off my boots, I wrapped myself
firmly in the old velvet curtain.

I looked longingly at the broken four-poster bed—no,
I could not face the prospect of trying to sleep on it.
I thought of mice and rats who no doubt had nests in the
ancient mattress. Ugh!

More important, I wanted to keep an eye on the loch
in case the monster returned to the island. I trembled,
not only from the intense cold but because I was afraid
to sleep.

The slightest noise . . .

But this time it was only the wind hurling itself against
the walls. My teeth were chattering with cold, my face
icy. I tried walking, waving my arms like windmills to

keep my blood from freezing. I soon had to give that up because there were too many loose boards for safety. The floor swayed beneath my feet, creaking at every step, moving like the floor at a fun-fair house. I hoped the room wouldn't collapse under me before morning!

Returning to my perch, I settled down as best I could. The minutes dragged; the stillness was so complete that I could have sworn that time itself had stopped.

I could have believed that the world beyond the tiny island had died, if the silence had not been broken briefly by signs of life from the distant shore. A dog barked, an owl hooted, then a shooting star, which at any other time I would have thought so romantic, dropped from the sky and was lost in space. A plane coming in to land somewhere to the north made me think fondly of overheated airports, of crowds of people, of life and warmth and everywhere so much food to eat.

There were signs of life from across the dark waters of the loch. The headlights of cars moving on some road several miles away. Families going home to warm beds and mugs of hot chocolate.

Sounds carry at night and a church clock chimed. But I forgot to count. It didn't make much difference to me what time it was until daybreak when all my hopes were pinned on attracting attention from Lochroy village.

I closed my eyes and yawned wearily. I thought I would never sleep. Worn out by the day's events, curled up on my hard window seat, wrapped in that dusty velvet curtain, I drifted away. I awoke hours later. Daybreak came with a lot of noise. Birds calling, distant farm animals demanding food, and the buzz of farm tractors.

I didn't exactly leap with joy at still being alive. I felt awful. I would have given away even that precious goblet, the cause of all my misfortunes, for a cup of coffee or even a glass of water. Instead I had to tell my unhappy stomach to stop complaining and wait while I considered what to do next.

Staring across that now peaceful sunlit stretch of water to Lochroy, my meeting last night with the monster from the deep seemed impossible and unreal. It could not have happened. I must have dreamed it. All I wanted now was to tell someone, have them nod and say yes, it had happened to them and no, I wasn't going mad dreaming up monsters and dead bodies from floating logs.

I thought about yesterday—the missing professor on the train and finding his spectacles by the lochside. The two men I was sure were crooks, chasing me in Corriedon. It all became more and more like some hideous nightmare.

But with daylight it was also time to see whether the goblet had survived. I took the wooden box from my backpack and carefully opened it. The goblet lay firmly in its faded velvet padding. I took it out gently and examined it. It had survived the last twenty-four hours in perfect condition and, considering the awful journey, much better than I had.

Replacing it, I began to wonder for the first time if there was a curse on it. Was it to blame for all my misfortunes? When I thought of the tragic life of its first owner, Mary, Queen of Scots, such an idea was not too hard to believe. Did it carry bad luck or death for anyone who had it in their possession?

Well, for more reasons than the money, I'd be glad to hand it over. The sooner the better!

I stood up carefully, sore and aching in every limb, to find that taking off my boots last night was a bad mistake. My sprained ankle was swollen, and I had a very painful struggle getting the boot on again. As I limped around by the windows, the ruined bedroom looked more ghastly than ever by daylight.

Worst of all, my hopes that the boat had been carried back to me by the current were soon dashed. The shore was empty.

And then I saw something. There was already traffic on the loch: a man in a boat. I waited no longer.

Hobbling down the staircase, I scrambled out of the door, through the nettles onto the far side of the island. I began waving my jacket and shouting. I had to attract his attention. This might be my only chance. The sailing season was over and there might not be any other boats on the loch that day.

Besides, if what I had seen last night in the loch was true, then I doubted whether the local fisherman would care to compete with a monster at night for a few trout.

As the boat came within range, I realize that the rower had his back toward me. As I yelled, I just hoped and prayed that he wasn't also playing a radio at full blast. If I lost him, I did not think I could survive another day without food and another freezing night on the island. And although I'm a good swimmer, I didn't want to take my chances in the icy waters of the loch, even without a monster on the prowl.

But my luck was in. He saw me, and I gabbled about losing my rowboat. Ten minutes later I was snugly squeezed among a huge pile of packages and parcels. This, I was told proudly, was the local delivery service, and his name was Len.

"Why don't you go by road?"

The boatman laughed and nodded toward the heavy load. "You haven't seen the road round the loch, have you, miss? Well, it's easier and quicker for me to get to the castle by water.

"They own all the land around this side of the loch and someday when they have made enough money from their tourist ventures, maybe they'll spend some of it providing a decent road."

He was curious to know how I had traveled. When I told him about Jock and the bus at Corriedon, he groaned. "That bus is always breaking down."

I said I had expected the Stuarts to collect me and had left a message.

He laughed. "We're lucky to have phones that work here. The electricity is a bit dicey at the best of times. As for that other answering thing you mentioned—" He shook his head sadly at anyone putting their trust in machines that talked back to you.

He found the story of my night in the island's ruined castle very funny.

Funny indeed, I thought. *Heartless wretch.* However, when he produced a flask of coffee and sandwiches, I forgave him. I told him about finding the rowboat at Corriedon, hoping the owner wouldn't be too upset when he got my note.

Len was suddenly grave. "You were lucky, miss. Nobody ever crosses the loch at night, miss," he said, looking over his shoulder and dropping his voice to a whisper, almost as if he might be overheard.

When I asked him why not, he thought for a moment before replying, "Currents, miss. They can be dangerous."

I looked at him. "What about the monster? Is he dangerous too?"

He avoided my eyes. "If he exists, then I suppose he might be dangerous."

"What about the two people who disappeared?"

"Who would they be, miss?" he asked cautiously.

When I said it was in all the papers, he shrugged. "The loch is very deep; it's never been charted. They could still be down there, trapped in underwater caverns."

"What about divers? Surely they sent divers down to look for them."

"I expect they did. But no man—no diver, that is—has ever reached the bottom of the loch."

Remembering what I had seen, I could think of one other very good reason why no diver wanted to tackle the depths of the loch. When Len saw my nervous expression, he said lightly, "You're not serious, miss. A bright young woman from a great big city like Edinburgh? You surely don't believe in such things as monsters."

"As a matter of fact, I did think I saw something last night."

"That would be most likely a floating tree trunk. There's a lot of them about. We had a big storm last month and trees from the island were blown down into the loch."

And without giving me any chance to comment, he pointed back to the island and said, "That old ruin was the original Castle Roy. The present one which you'll see as we turn around the bend dates from the time of Queen Victoria—"

As he spoke, I realized that the loch was bigger than I had first thought. Instead of going straight across from the island to the village, we were making a big loop to the left and heading westward.

"Aren't we going the wrong way to the castle?"

Len laughed at my ignorance. "This is the quickest way, miss, if you don't have a car. It's a mile or so down the drive, and the castle folk decided that the tourists would like the idea of arriving by boat. Romantic, like being back in the old days, so they had the causeway repaired at the back of the castle. And there it is now—"

Only battlements with a flag flying were visible through the trees. A long, sloping lawn and a lot of dark bushes lay in between. After helping me ashore, Len took out the parcels and boxes, piled them in a wooden shed by the pier, and began loading the boat with packages left by the Stuarts for his return journey.

Meanwhile I looked around hopefully for whoever would be arriving to collect the new supplies and take me up to the castle.

When I mentioned this, he said, "Miss Stuart will come for them in her car later, sometime when she's doing the rounds."

"And when is that?"

"I couldn't tell you. Might not be till late afternoon. I wouldn't be waiting if I were you. It's no distance to walk," he added, giving me directions:

"Straight across the grass here, take the path to the left, then right, then straight ahead for two hundred yards, then left again, second right, and you'll come out on the drive."

It was all very bewildering. But before I could ask him to repeat it, he had cast off and with a cheery wave was rowing from the shore. As I stood watching him, utterly confused, wishing I had time to write it all down, he called, "You can't get lost."

Couldn't I? He didn't know me or my sense of direction. It was bad enough in a city like Edinburgh which I had known all my life, well supplied with landmarks, like spires and domes and signposts. But here in this bewildering array of greenery, bushes, and paths that all looked alike, I was doomed.

After finding myself back at the causeway for the second time, feeling angry and tired, I sat down. I took the map from my backpack but it was utterly useless. There were no estate roads marked and it showed only the village and the castle.

Taking a deep breath, I started off again. One half mile and one half hour later, my sprained right ankle began to protest. Why hadn't I thought to bring that stick with me? I tried to remember Len's directions. Another look at the map's contour lines suggested that if I left this greenery, there was a very steep hill between me and the castle.

The fence I leaned against circled an empty, flat field. In one corner above the trees, I could see a glimpse of a flag and the castle battlements. That's where I would head, and I waited no longer. I climbed over, walked about fifty yards into the field, and found it was no longer empty.

The other occupant was a mean-looking Highland beast, all shaggy red hair and a good deal of it over its eyes. There were also two evil-looking sharp horns which were moving briskly toward me as I limped quickly back toward that fence.

There was no doubt in my mind that the beast's increased pace meant business. I made it just in time to put the fence between us. He glared at me, snorted noisily in case I intended to re-enter his pasture.

I was very weary and very depressed. Being chased by a Highland beast was the last straw. How on earth was I to get through to a castle as cleverly hidden as Sleeping Beauty's palace? However, I decided that by walking around the outside of the field, I might be lucky enough to land somewhere on the castle drive.

Off I went, followed at a distance and closely watched by the Highland beast. It didn't take long to find that going around a field was easier in theory than in reality. Every now and again my progress was halted by wild bushes and paths that sloped away in the opposite direction.

Then at last, I saw a gleam of gray. A roof. Hurrah! I had found a house in the forest like a princess in a fairy tale.

This house was a sort of mini-castle, tiny but all battlements, turrets, and arched windows. The rooms inside must have been no larger than cupboards—a brave attempt at being romantic and different. The whole building could have been lifted up and removed on a good-sized truck.

There was a clearing behind the house, a stretch of garden. The cottage was probably occupied by the Stuarts' servants. At least they would be able to point me in the right direction since my ankle was so painful now that I couldn't walk much farther. Perhaps they would even take pity on my distress and like some miracle produce a car. Anything to transport me at that moment would have seemed like a gift from heaven.

And then as I came nearer, I heard it. A dog barked loudly. It wasn't a welcome-glad-you-came bark. There was a warning ring about it.

Should I go on, risk the owner being at home, and hope the dog was firmly chained?

I was almost at the door when a second dog barked, then a third. I waited no longer and hurried back along the path as fast as I could go. Plunging once more into the shelter of the greenery, I felt safe for the time being.

Then I saw the notice: "Castle Roy Kennels."

I gave a sigh of relief. The noisy dogs I had heard would be chained up, of course. Silly me, being so scared. I should go back and knock at the door. The kennel owner would surely laugh at my being such a coward.

Only I didn't go after all. I lost my nerve once more. And I had thought of something. Kennels suggested that dogs were transported in their owners' cars. And that meant the castle drive must be nearby.

Pleased with myself, I limped on. The noise of the dogs was stilled.

Thank heaven for that. And at last, a gravel path. To my delight it came out within sight of the back entrance to the castle. What I took to be the kitchen door was just thirty yards away across the clearing.

Wait a moment, those dogs were barking again! Near at hand, growing nearer. Too close now for my peace of mind.

I began limping toward the door when from the greenery behind me, a pack of the largest, blackest dogs I had ever seen rushed out. All of them were big enough and fierce enough to make Calum's Nero appear as gentle as a lamb.

They lifted their heads, got my scent, and raced toward me, baying. I yelled out as I staggered wildly toward the castle and safety.

Then with a growl, the leader of the pack was on me. As I fell to the ground, screaming, I heard a voice, "Seize her—seize her!"

CHAPTER 9

I opened my eyes and closed them hastily again. I realized I was still alive, but where was I? Nothing hurt and I still had my arms and legs intact. I hadn't been attacked by a pack of fierce dogs. I kept my eyes open this time.

There was a sigh of relief. "Are you all right, miss?"

A human voice and a rather gentle one. It belonged to a big, tall man in a faded tartan kilt. He was built like a barn door, with the sort of wild hair you see only in films of Highlanders rushing into battle: thick, black, and curly. The rest of his features were lost behind a beard that matched his hair. It gave me an odd feeling that a pair of fierce black eyes was watching me through a thick hairy hedge.

He grinned. "Sorry you got such a fright, miss." Pausing, he shouted to a large black dog heading briskly toward me, "You're all wet! Seize her—seize her!"

I screamed and hid my head. "No—no, please, leave me alone."

"What ails you, miss?" I opened my eyes and he was stroking the big black dog's head. "He wouldn't hurt anyone, he's only curious. Just had his morning swim. Can't keep him out of water. But he's gentle as a lamb, aren't you, Caesar?"

I knew all about dogs that were gentle as lambs.

The hairy man was puzzled. Suddenly he laughed. "I get it now. 'Caesar—seize her.' Well, if that doesn't beat everything—"

And throwing back his head he roared with mirth. "You thought I was saying 'Seize her.' That's his name, just sounds the same: C-a-e-s-a-r." He spelled it out. "You know, like the old Roman emperor."

I nodded weakly. I was on familiar ground with Roman emperors. Their names had to be favorites for folks who owned big, fierce dogs. First Calum's Nero and now Caesar.

"He's a German hunting dog," said Caesar's owner proudly. "One of the largest of the breed."

I could believe that. And for one moment I thought fondly of that other dog back home in Edinburgh. In size, Nero could have been this big dog's baby brother.

"Rory's my name, miss. Rory Stuart."

"You are one of the Castle Stuarts?"

"No, no, lass. I only work for them. No kin at all. We all have the same name here. You'd be hard pressed to find anyone at Lochroy who isn't called Stuart."

"Like Smith?" I said. Smith was the name Dad used in his business deals. Just for income tax purposes, he said, so as not to get the bookshop involved. But I had my own ideas about that.

Rory laughed. "Now, miss, come inside and rest a minute. It's the least we can do after scaring you. Would you like something to drink? A wee dram, perhaps?"

"Not at this hour, thank you. But ask me later," I said as I followed him and Caesar inside a tiny cottage and sat on the sofa. I was no longer scared of this gentle giant, whatever his early morning drinking habits.

He was looking puzzled. He and his dog studied me as if I were a new species who had landed in their parlor. Caesar even wagged his tail. Head on one side, he watched me with an almost human expression. Calum would have told me he was saying he was sorry.

Rory went over to the sideboard, took a bottle, and held it out for my inspection. "You're sure?"

"Absolutely no whisky, thank you, Mr. Stuart—"

"Rory," he said, pouring himself a generous measure.

"I'm Annie."

We shook hands solemnly and I said, "I would love a glass of water."

"Water? Really?" That took him by surprise, as if I'd asked for something exotic and rare. And shaking his head rather sadly, he carried his bottle into what I presumed was the kitchen.

I looked around. I was seated on a sofa in a small room with an arched window like something out of a church. It was a cozy, rather shabby, but comfortable room. A sideboard was weighed down with Victorian china dogs, ornaments, and family photographs. There were dainty hunting prints on the walls.

I had an idea I was looking at the original wallpaper of faded roses—at least a hundred years out of date. I liked it. The room had a feeling of rest and peace. But it had never been built or furnished with a giant like Rory in mind.

He would have to duck his head every time he went through any of the doors. It must have given him a sore neck. He came back with a jug and carefully measured out a small glass of water.

I looked around. "Where am I?" I asked. But I had already worked that out. I sniffed the air. It didn't require any powers of detection to guess that I was on the inside of Castle Roy Kennels.

If I needed further proof, the room had a doggy smell. As if they were used to making themselves at home with Rory on the sofa and the chairs.

Rory nodded. "This is the kennels, miss. Castle Roy Kennels. Are you feeling better now? When Caesar ran up to you, you yelled out and fell down. I thought you maybe knocked yourself out when you bumped your head. Is it sore?"

There was a very tender spot where I had hit the ground. "It's not too bad," I said bravely, gulping down my glass of water. It tasted so good. "More please."

He watched me, trying not to wince as I drank. "Sure you don't want something in it? To take away the taste, I mean?"

He was surprised and a bit shocked, as if he'd caught me at drugs. How someone could enjoy fresh clean water was beyond him. It also accounted for the tiny glass that was now empty.

I held it up. "Best taste in the whole world."

He shrugged, obviously not sharing my good opinion of Highland water. Didn't he know that people in supermarkets all over the world pay good money to buy it in large bottles?

He thought for a moment, then asked politely: "Lost, were you?"

"Something like that. But thank you for your help." I tried to stand up.

I cried out and Rory caught me.

"It's my ankle."

"Sit down, miss. Sit down and I'll have a wee look at it. You can't go hiking around this part of the world without two good strong feet. How did it happen?"

As he spoke he went into the tiny kitchen and returned with a basin of warm water. Kneeling down, he undid my laces and removed my boot and sock. Then with hands very gentle indeed, he carefully examined my ankle.

"Nothing broken, miss. Just a wee sprain, that's all. It'll be fine. I'll bind it up for you—a day or two resting it and you'll be leaping about again."

I doubted that but I sat back and looked down on that tousled head. He would be older than Dad. I decided he was like the water—simply gorgeous! I love gentle giants and if I'd been looking for a father figure, I would have fallen in love with him then and there.

The bandage firmly fixed, he sat back on his heels and looked up at me, "Try it now."

I stood up gingerly and he held my arm. It hardly hurt at all. "It's great," I said. "What would I have done if I hadn't met you?"

He grinned again. "It's all in the day's work. I'm used to looking after dogs and horses. Animals get hurt feet and legs. They have accidents too. If I'd had the chance, I'd have trained as a vet. I've worked with animals all my life."

He sighed. "My father worked for the old Stuarts. When he died, I just stayed on. They wanted someone to run the kennels, and I do odd jobs about the place."

Pausing, he studied my face again. It was a puzzled look as if something bothered him and he was trying to work it out. "Where are you staying, miss?"

"Annie," I reminded him. I told him I had come across from Corriedon with the boatman.

He grinned. "My cousin Len. So you've met him. Well, well." He made it sound as if we were now old friends.

"I was going to the castle—" I stopped. I suddenly remembered the goblet, the cause of all my problems. I panicked.

"I had a backpack with me—" I tried to sound calm. "Where is it?"

He nodded. "It's over there by the door. See? That's the bathroom—"

"Thank you," I said gratefully.

The bathtub was a joy to behold. It belonged in a museum. Painted green, it had huge claw-like feet. It was like the lower half of a dinosaur scooped out and put to good use as a bath. Even if there had been hot water coming from the faucets instead of icy cold, I would have had second thoughts about using the tub and lowering myself into that bath's gloomy depths.

There were fewer risks attached to using the washbasin. It was of the same antique era with fancy brass handles. The toilet with a chain that, when pulled, sounded like the rattling of a whole army of ghosts.

Ten minutes later I emerged feeling rosy, thanks to the chilly water. I was clean and tidy, ready to face the day and, hopefully, Dad's client, Mr. Jones. He should be there waiting for me to hand over the goblet to him.

Rory looked at me, nodded in approval. He had noticed the difference a wash and brushup can make. For a moment he looked as if he were going to say something important. He opened his mouth, closed it again, and shook his head. "No matter. Going to the castle, are you?"

"Yes."

"I thought you were a hiker."

I didn't know what to say, so I shook my head rather vaguely.

Rory got the wrong idea. "Looking for work, are you?"

"They're expecting me."

He nodded. "The tourist season's over. They needed help weeks ago. I told them then but they're stubborn. Think they know it all—"

I didn't know what to say, how much to tell my rescuer.

There was a feeling of caution, a warning bell ringing at the back of my mind. I didn't know what it was then, but I was to find out later. I acted purely on my instinct for danger. There were other times in my life I had followed my instinct, and I had been proved right.

So I would keep quiet about what I was doing here, my mission to Castle Roy. Perhaps the events of the last twenty-four hours were to blame. Could it be only yesterday since I had left Edinburgh station?

I had expected a pleasant train journey, a bus to Castle Roy to be met by the Stuarts. When business was completed, I expected a chance to explore before returning. What had I found instead? Not one thing about this journey was what it seemed. Beware of taking things for granted at first sight, I decided. A fellow traveler, the professor, had disappeared. Two men who thought I knew him were eager to include me in their grim activities.

I told myself: remember the missing Dr. Parker and his spectacles you found on the shore of the loch at

Corriedon. That's what happens when you don't mind your own business. You end up stranded on an island in the middle of nowhere with a monster in the loch and a load of trouble on your hands.

By all accounts, that was all behind me now. I had arrived at Castle Roy with a sprained ankle but my goblet had survived intact. I could relax now. All would be well with Dad's client waiting for me. Mr. Jones—if that was his real name was none of my concern, as long as he handed over the money as specified on my copy of the document of agreement.

But still at the back of my mind, refusing to budge, was this nagging feeling that my troubles were just about to begin. The curtain was about to rise on Act II.

And the name of it was "Deadly Danger."

CHAPTER
10

I followed Rory Stuart out of the cottage to the back of the castle. The dogs came with us. I thought, *Calum will never believe this! If he could see me now with the dogs trotting alongside like something from a Disney film!*

Rory tried the kitchen door. It was locked.

He seemed surprised, tried it again, and swore under his breath.

"Something wrong?" I said.

He scratched his ear. "They've started locking it at night. Getting nervous in their old age. Prowlers and so forth." He laughed a little off-key, I thought, as if the Stuarts weren't the only ones concerned about break-ins.

It was my turn to be surprised. This seemed to be the last place I'd have expected prowlers, a breed I associated with city suburbs.

Rory sighed deeply. "I'll take you in by the front door. I have to get the key first."

"Isn't there a bell you could ring?"

"A bell!" He laughed at that. "What would they want with a bell? The door's never been locked as long as I can remember. Nobody ever locks doors in this part of the world, especially kitchen doors."

He sighed again. "I suppose it's all this rubbish talk that encourages strangers—" He stopped suddenly.

I asked, "What rubbish talk?"

He shrugged. "Oh, nothing."

"You mean about the monster in the loch?" I said casually.

He stared at me. "How—how did—?"

I laughed. "I read the papers too, you know."

He looked relieved. "Wait here," he said, and he turned to go back to the cottage.

I shook my head and walked with him. He made no comment.

I just didn't want to wait alone. The dogs were there, of course, and it wasn't because I was afraid of them. Now that they had sniffed me over and scared the life out of me, I was of no further interest to them. They had had their fun for the day.

It was something else that bothered me. The early morning light held no threat. There was a faint mist still lying on the loch, the promise of warmth in thin sunlight. By all accounts it was going to be a very nice day. I could breathe again with all the terrors of the night behind me. I was safe at last, my mission almost over.

By tomorrow I'd be on my way to Edinburgh, to Calum and Dad. They would be frantic by now at not having heard from me.

At the cottage, I asked, "May I make a phone call, please? Just a brief one," I added.

"Sure, miss. I'll need to search for that spare key to the front door. I haven't seen it in ages. Can't remember when I last used it—kitchen door has always been handier for me."

"Why do they lock the front door and leave the back door open?" It didn't make sense to me, if it was burglars they were afraid of.

"Och, it's just during the tourist season. They have to be careful. You never know what kind of people—"

Pausing, he looked at me, a little embarrassed. It was my kind of people—the hitchhikers, the backpackers, and passing strangers—he meant who might be dangerous. An open door might be an invitation to lift some of the silver or anything of value.

I went into the room we had just left and dialed the bookshop. There was no reply.

That was odd. Dad opened the door as the clock at St. Giles Cathedral struck nine o'clock every morning. He got into a panic at being late. As if customers might be forming a line outside the door, their lives depending on buying one of his books.

I tried the house number. There was no reply. I put down the phone, trying not to feel worried. I told myself that Susie was giving him breakfast at the bakery.

Then I dialed Calum's number. A very businesslike lady told me this was the police and asked which emergency service I needed.

I explained that this was a personal call and she didn't like that. She said rather coldly that she would try to connect me. Her tone indicated that I shouldn't pin my hopes on it, though. As my call was sent from one office to the other with a lot of rather long intervals, I waited patiently, expecting to hear Calum's cheery voice any moment.

And with nothing better to do, I stared at the smiling group photographs on the wall. I also had time to work out what this call was going to cost at this time of the day before I reached the right department.

At last! But I was told that Detective Sergeant Crail was in a meeting. Would I leave a message?

"Just tell him that Miss Kelty called from Lochroy. I'll call him later."

Rory came in rattling the keys. "Found them. Hold on a wee minute, miss, until I lock up the dogs. They're allowed in the kitchen but not in the other parts of the house. And please put that back in your purse!" he added pointing to the money I'd put down for the call.

I went to the door and waited for him, wishing I could shake off this feeling of unease. It was like a sour taste in my mouth and there was no logical reason for it. The hills were stirring sleepily under a thin mist. A flock of sheep made gentle background noises. I could tell myself I had dreamed about the monster—seeing the head and neck, the eyes and ferocious mouth, seeing it swimming toward me, hearing it breathe—

I shuddered. Even to think of last night turned my blood to ice. I shook my head as if to force such dark thoughts away forever. It couldn't be real. There was no room for such nonsense in practical Edinburgh. Or here in Lochroy at nine in the morning with only the gentle country sounds and the wine clear air.

But I couldn't escape. I couldn't shake off that feeling of lurking danger, real as a whispered word in the soft breeze from the hills covered with heather. Like a ghostly hand raised in silent warning.

The silence was broken by Rory's cheery voice from the kennels, telling them to be good dogs. Why on earth should I have that prickling sense of disaster? Surely there was nothing sinister about this kind man who was taking care of me.

And then I remembered that I was part Highland too, although my father tended to forget his roots. I felt as if I had made an interesting discovery. Then suddenly I knew what was bothering me.

The phone calls. That was it! Being unable to reach Dad or Calum had made me anxious and uneasy.

I though about the old-fashioned phone on that ancient cluttered sideboard. While I waited I had studied the photographs on the wall above. Black-and-white, sepia, old photos that belonged to the time before we had color. Children, old people, smiling happy couples. A group of servants sitting on the front steps of the castle.

There was a face—

"Ready to face the foe?" I jumped. Rory was back and he led the way around to the front of the castle. Across a gravel path and through a kitchen garden with greenhouses. The grapevines, once the pride and joy of earlier Stuarts, had withered long ago. The walled garden was a sad sight. Nothing but a few bleak rows of vegetables in desperate need of tender loving care.

Rory said, "Mrs. Stuart will be glad to see you. They had guests last night for a golden wedding dinner so I expect that's why they're not up and about this morning. There's always a lot of clearing up—"

But I wasn't listening. Rory had got my arrival at the castle all wrong. Although I expected to find Mr. Jones waiting for me, some instinct told me to be cautious. The fewer people who knew who I was, the better. Until we actually met, I would be wise to keep quiet about my reason for being here with that valuable goblet in my backpack.

Later, I realized that my guardian angel must have been working unpaid overtime that morning.

The front of the castle looked like many of the others I had glimpsed on the train journey across the Highlands. Turrets and battlements hinted at a brave past with battles fought and won long ago—a kind of King Arthur's Camelot where his Knights of the Round Table would have been no great surprise.

I remembered that, seen from the island on the loch, Castle Roy had looked very grand indeed. Now a close-up view showed the flaws. The condition of the stone walls suggested that there wasn't much money here. Paying guests obviously didn't add enough to allow for a coat of paint, either. In fact, several coats of paint were badly needed on flaky woodwork.

I wondered how many of those other grand castles would have stood up to a closer inspection. The flag above the battlements indicated that the Stuarts were in residence. But it was all rather sad and depressing.

Following Rory past a couple of very worn stone lions, long past scaring any intruder, I patted their heads and asked, "Is it haunted? Is there a resident ghost?"

Rory looked startled and then he laughed: "Not that I've ever heard of!"

His mirth indicated that it was a silly question, so I said, "Tell me about the Stuarts."

"There isn't much to tell, miss. Mrs. Faith Stuart and Miss Hope Stuart are sisters. Mrs. Faith married a Stuart cousin, so she didn't change her surname."

"Where's Mr. Stuart?"

"Dead, miss, these ten years. An accident on the loch."

"How sad. What happened?"

Rory looked thoughtful. "Drowned. Boat overturned. Sudden storm—the loch can be treacherous. Happens in this part of the world."

I nodded. I had some experience of that last night. I wanted to know more about that accident, but Rory's abrupt manner said that he didn't want to dwell on unpleasant subjects.

Faith and Hope. These Stuart kinships were baffling. "Is there a Charity, by any chance?" I asked.

Rory looked amazed. "There is indeed. How did you guess?" When I merely smiled, he said, "Miss Charity— well, like Hope she never married. She keeps to herself most of the time these days."

"Is she ill?"

He thought about that before replying, "Just in her poor mind."

Unlocking the door, he ushered me into a huge hall with a grand staircase winding its way upward—an opulent staircase, the kind for the Ziegfeld girls or Scarlett O'Hara. It was the most impressive part of Castle Roy, a first sight bound to impress tourist guests before they saw the rest of the house.

On our right, an open door led into a huge, rather shabby room with handsome windows overlooking the loch. A flagged terrace hinted at afternoon teas in the sunshine.

There were runners of threadbare blue-green tartan carpet and in the center of the floor, a large table and dining chairs. At the foot of each chair sat a hassock in matching tartan. I guessed this was a necessity to keep the diners' feet from freezing on stone floors.

Across the corridor was the drawing room whose enormous stone fireplace was an exact copy of the one

I had seen in the ruined castle on the island. Intended for burning huge logs in happier days, it now held a rather boring electric fire. The sagging sofas were covered by the same faded tartan as the furnishings in the dining room.

Closing my eyes, I had a terrible vision. A flight into the future, a hundred years from now when Castle Roy would also be a deserted ruin with one wall standing, looking like the one on the island.

There was a feeling of great sadness around us. I thought about the three sisters—Faith, Hope, and Charity—and decided they must belong to a bygone age too.

When I asked Rory, he grinned. "Fifty-ish, my age, if you call that old, miss."

"Of course not," I said hastily.

"But the Stuarts all live to a great age," he added with some satisfaction.

Unless they drown in the loch, I thought. *Or whatever is there gets to them first.*

CHAPTER 11

"I see you're admiring our tartan furnishings," said Rory.

Admiring was far from the truth, but I didn't want to hurt his feelings.

I smiled. "They must have got a bargain lot."

Rory looked solemn. "You're right. The castle isn't as old as it tries to look, you know. Built in the 1880s, when everyone with any money and a bit of land was crazy to have a house that looked like Balmoral Castle. The Queen went overboard for tartan and so did everyone else. I reckon it has faded with age."

That made it just livable. In mint condition it must have been pretty awful.

"Old Angus Stuart was a financier. A crafty old devil too. Come and I'll show you."

He led the way to the fireplace. "Look up the chimney yonder."

I craned my neck and stared upward into the gloom. "See that square of light half way up there? That's the Laird's Lug. Built specially for Angus."

As we ducked back into the room, he said, "The room directly above this was old Angus's study. Angus was the *laird*, the *lord*, of this castle. He used to invite business rivals to stay, and after dinner he would retire to his room. He pretended to be a bit of an invalid. He would rush upstairs and listen to them talking about him. And giving away a lot of useful information about their business plans."

He stopped and looked at me. "It still works. You can hear every word. You know what a *lug* is, don't you, Annie?" he said, tweaking his ear.

As if I hadn't lived in Edinburgh all my life and not known that *lugs* were *ears*.

I followed him down the corridor where he opened a very creaky door.

We were in the kitchen. It had won no prize for design in this century: gas brackets, stone floor, black-leaded range, and gas stove which looked like an original model. But it worked, for there was a delicious smell of baking and fresh coffee.

Two large women in huge aprons and white caps had their backs to us. I thought I was seeing wax models, put there by the Stuarts. A special exhibit to let guests know what the kitchen looked like more than a hundred years ago.

Suddenly they moved. Two pairs of round brown eyes in round pale faces regarded us, solemn as owls.

"Mrs. Faith Stuart and Miss Hope Stuart, this is Annie."

Rory smiled. "I brought her over to give you a hand. We came in by the front door."

"You came by the front door," Mrs. Stuart, elder and stouter of the two, repeated. She gave him a dirty look. Then she scanned me from tip to toe, very slowly. Her deep sigh said plainer than any words that I didn't look like a guest.

"The kitchen door was locked," said Rory.

"Locked—?"

Hope put a warning hand on her sister's arm. "Yes, Rory. It's safer that way."

Rory bowed slightly. "As you wish." And to me, "I'll leave you here, Annie."

Mrs. Stuart had never taken her eyes off me. "We can't offer you anything at the moment. I'm afraid you're too late for the tourist season."

"We *are* expecting a guest, Faith. The American gentleman," said her sister.

That sounded like Mr. Jones. But surely he should have been here already waiting for me. Where was he?

As if I had asked the question, Hope said, "Mr. Jones has been delayed."

Damn, damn—I groaned inwardly.

"The post office brought a message up from him," said Hope. "From the airport."

Why didn't he phone them himself? I wondered.

"I'm sorry, miss," said Faith, looking at me. "We can't afford staff at the moment. Whoever gave you the information got it wrong. You should have consulted us first before coming all this way for nothing."

Hope looked at her. "But Mr. Jones should be here

shortly. There's this important date with a gentleman from Edinburgh."

Faith frowned. "Who seems to be delayed as well. It can hardly be the weather to blame. We don't even have snow yet. It's all very annoying."

It was indeed, and confusing too. I had a quick think. Obviously they hadn't got my message on the answering machine. But I thought Dad had told them before I left Edinburgh to expect me. The lines were badly crossed somewhere, and it looked as if the whole system had broken down.

"Where are you heading for?" asked Hope, who had taken my silence as disappointment at not getting a job at the castle. "You might still get work in some of the hotels on Deeside or in Inverness," she added helpfully

"Yes—thanks. I'll try them," I said.

I was glad I hadn't revealed my identity. I could not shake off that sense of warning, that absurd feeling of danger. So I'd play my hunch, hang around on some excuse, pretend to be the girl looking for work as a servant until Mr. Jones arrived.

All I had to do was wait a few hours. I would hand over the goblet to him, get the money, and head for home again.

It would only be a couple of days. It was simple. Dead simple. Or put it another way. Simply dead. And I almost was.

"There isn't a bus until tomorrow morning. There's only one a day. The school bus—" said Hope.

I knew it well.

"You'll need somewhere to stay," she added with a look in her sister's direction.

"We'll need the two bedrooms for our guests when they arrive. The suites aren't at all suitable as servants' quarters," said Faith stiffly. And as if I wasn't present, she added, "I suppose she could sleep in Angus's study."

"There isn't a proper bed, Faith. Just a sofa," said Hope.

Faith frowned, looked me over, decided that I looked as if I might have slept rough before.

Since I had to be there when Mr. Jones arrived, whatever the hour, I said hastily, "That'll be fine. It's only for one night. What time is the school bus?"

Hope gave me the time and I wondered if Jock had got the bus fixed yet, when she added, "You get a connection to Inverness from Glenmohr."

I took up my backpack and she led the way up the grand staircase to what Rory had described as the "laird's lug."

As soon as I stepped inside that tiny room above the drawing room, I decided that it was haunted. The walls were paneled in dark oak. It would be like sleeping in a box only a few shades bigger than Dracula's coffin.

There wasn't much in the way of furniture either—an old desk, firmly padlocked, and a threadbare armchair and sofa. Its plush covering didn't quite hide bulging springs. I was in for another restless night. At least it would be safe and slightly more comfortable than the window seat in the ruined castle on the island.

"Bathroom's next door. Can you find your way down to the kitchen again?"

"Yes. How much is this going to cost me?"

"I've no idea. You'll need to ask Faith. She deals with the business side."

Alone, I sat down on the sofa and thought what to do next. I couldn't carry the goblet everywhere so I must find some safe hiding place. There was nothing visible in the room except the fireplace. I remembered the chimney and looked inside. I could see light from the drawing room below and a ledge about two feet down.

It looked a safe enough storage place for the wooden box. At least no one would think of looking for it there. I went to wash the soot from the old fireplace off my hands. This bathroom I guessed was seldom used. The monstrous bathtub had green moss growing in its base. The toilet had seen cleaner days too.

Back in the study, I decided I must find a phone and call Dad and Calum. But not from here. The fact that the post office carried messages for the castle suggested that their phone didn't work any better than the answering machine.

But most of all, I didn't want to be overheard. I decided there was sure to be a public phone in the village.

Downstairs in the kitchen, Faith was peeling vegetables, getting ready for the two gentlemen who would be arriving, she hoped, in time for dinner.

I told her I must send some postcards.

"We don't have any postcards." She looked me over again as if this was an unusual request.

Hope emerged from one of the deep cupboards which was bigger than the study I was to sleep in. "There's a post office in the village. Rory mentioned that you hurt your ankle," she added.

"It's a long walk down the drive," said Faith. "Hope can take you down when she goes across the gardens in the van to collect our supplies from Len."

"Len comes across the loch by boat," Hope explained.

I knew all about Len and the boat, but I merely nodded and said, "I'd really enjoy the walk."

"Are you sure?" Hope said doubtfully. "There's a bike in the shed. I'll get it—"

"It's Charity's bike," said her sister sharply.

Hope smiled. "She won't mind."

"That would be great, if it's all right," I said.

"It's vintage 1930 but it's in good working order."

"You will take care of it, won't you?" said Faith severely.

I promised to do so.

"Since you're going to the village, there are one or two things—" Faith wrote a list and signed it as Hope returned with the bike. "They know me," she said. "Tell them I'll be in to pay the bill later."

As they anxiously watched me wobbling away from the kitchen door and on to the drive, I wondered, *Was all this just a test of my honesty, to make sure they'd see both me and the bike again?*

My ankle protested at this old-fashioned pedal bicycle, but I was glad I wasn't walking and thankful that I reached Lochroy without falling off.

The post office also served as general store. And beside it was the best sight in the world for me: a pay phone.

I dialed the operator and said I wanted to call collect. Two minutes later Dad had approved and I was speaking to him.

Without as much as "How are you?" his first question was, "Have you delivered the goblet? Did you get the money all right?"

When I explained that Mr. Jones had been delayed, Dad groaned. He sounded annoyed, as I knew he would be somehow. I said that they were expecting him anytime now.

"I've been very worried about you, Annie. I expected to hear from you last night."

"I tried to phone you at nine this morning. Where were you?"

"Right here in the shop. Where else would I be?" He sounded cross. "What happened to you, anyway?"

"I didn't get to the castle until this morning—there were delays—"

"Oh, I see." He didn't sound very concerned about my delays. "Journey all right apart from that?"

There just wasn't any answer to that one. I spared him the details. After all, he was paying for the call. "It's a long story. I'll tell you all about it when I get home. And before you go, Dad. The Stuarts have got the idea that you are coming personally to meet Mr. Jones."

There was silence. I thought he had hung up.

"Dad? Didn't you tell them that it was your daughter who was making the delivery?"

"Of course I did, Annie. I left a message on the answering machine."

"They never got it. It doesn't seem to work at all."

"That's a pity."

Across the miles, I heard the shop doorbell ring.

"Must go, Annie. A customer."

I knew. And the sound made me as homesick as I'd never been before.

"I'll let you know when I'll be home, after I've seen Mr. Jones," I said. "Tell Calum I called, will you?" The line went dead before I could leave a message for Calum.

As I bicycled through the castle gates, I thought over our conversation. There were a few things that didn't quite add up. Before I left Edinburgh, I distinctly remembered Dad saying that he had phoned the Stuarts. He had arranged for them to pick me up at the bus stop—

Because it was a long drive up to the castle!

Now, if he hadn't spoken to them personally but had left a message on the answering machine, how come he knew about the drive? Had he been here before? A thought—something I had seen—

Then suddenly a ghostly figure emerged from the shrubbery. A pale grey gown, a huge grey hat, ghostly arms waving—the grey lady of Castle Roy!

Rory had forgotten to tell me about her. And that she did her haunting in broad daylight. At eleven o'clock in the morning.

CHAPTER
12

The grey lady was no ghost. Waving arms or not, she was quite flesh and blood.

I wasn't sure whether I should bicycle on and pretend I hadn't seen her. However, she stood in front of me, barring the way.

"So you've come back. They told me you were dead."

Leaning closer, she peered at my face. "You're still alive—after all these years." She grinned. "I thought I was seeing a ghost. Gave me quite a turn, you did."

I couldn't think of an answer to that one.

"What are you doing here? This is MY castle and that is my bicycle. Who gave it to you?" As she spoke, she seized the handlebars and gave it—and me—a good shaking.

It seemed safer to get off. "I'm sorry. Would you like it back?" I asked, although she would never be able to bicycle in those clothes.

Her dress would scare anyone into thinking they were seeing a ghost. The grey chiffon dress. A picture hat. Grey gloves. Stockings and shoes. All belonged to the 1890s. I could see that her makeup was right for the spirit world too. Dead-white face powder!

"You must be Miss Charity," I said.

"So you do remember me."

"They told me about you. I'm Annie. I'm helping your sisters out for a while."

"What did they tell you about me?" she asked.

"Not a great deal. But I'm pleased to meet you."

I held out my hand. Her own was none too clean but it was real enough. "Weren't you scared? That I might be a ghost, I mean?"

She looked quite disappointed when I laughed. "In broad daylight, Miss Charity? Never!"

"Dammit," she said and stamped her foot in a very unghostlike manner. "Lots of people are absolutely terrified of me, you know."

I suspected she was a little mad, but the gleam in her eye meant business. As she held on to the bike, her nails were very long and sharply pointed. They were painted a very unghostly bright red. A vampire touch, I decided, to be extra scary.

As we walked along the drive together I asked, "Are you part of the tourist attraction, Miss Charity?"

"What do you mean?" she said indignantly. "Tourist attraction indeed!"

"The Grey Lady of Castle Roy. Like the monster in the loch."

She shivered and looked over her shoulder toward the loch. "No—not like *him*." She went on quickly: "I'm not really pretend, you know. Great-Grandma sometimes takes me over like she did when I was a little girl, telling me what she wants me to do. These are her clothes—"

Again that quick look behind us. "I'm not really—bad. Not like *him*."

"*Him?*"

She walked closer and whispered, almost as if she might be overheard. "You know, *him* over there. In the loch." And linking arms with me. "I saw you walking with Rory and the dogs. When he told me about how scared you were, I said you'd always been afraid of dogs."

Her laugh revealed rather long, fang-like teeth which hadn't been seen by a dentist in many years. They looked very strong and yellow against that pale mouth and thin lips. I tried not to shiver as I realized how scared I would have been if Rory hadn't warned me about Charity's poor sick mind.

"Rory's my greatest friend," she said. "He tells me all about what is going on up there." She pointed to the castle. "Miss Faith and Miss Hope despise me, you know. They think I let the side down, that I can never be a lady like them and go into good society. It worries them when their friends see me. They like to keep me out of sight."

Again that shrill laugh. "They've always been ashamed of me just because I didn't behave like them and saw things they couldn't see."

She was silent, very still, staring across towards the loch.

"What kind of things?" I asked gently.

"Oh, just—things, you know. Battles—men in armor fighting on horses. Other people call them ghosts, but that's just because they can't see them. They say I made it all up just because I wanted to live back in Great-Grandma's time when everything was different at the castle. When we had carriages to ride, and all the county came to our famous parties, and we had lovely ball gowns."

She stopped and spread the skirt of that dingy, grey chiffon dress. "Nicer than this one. But you always liked it so. I'm glad I decided to wear it today when I knew you were coming. Remember you altered it to fit me? Do you still sew? You were so good at that. And you said it made me look prettier than Miss Faith and Miss Hope. That made them so mad!" She paused to laugh again at her sisters' anger. "We both knew why, though, didn't we? They were jealous, afraid that the young men who came to call might want to marry me. They were afraid that they'd be left on the shelf for ever and ever—"

I was getting lost. Again she stopped and looked down into my face. "I always knew you would come back someday. They told me you were dead. You were always my favorite, you know. None of the maids could do my hair the way you did."

Although she smiled at me, it wasn't my face she was seeing now.

"Will you do my hair today?" She took off the hat and I saw a tangled web of grey hair that hadn't seen a comb or brush or a shampoo in a very long time. She ran her hands through it—with difficulty.

"You always did it so beautifully." She sighed. "'It's such a lovely color, Miss Charity,' you'd say. 'You have gorgeous hair. Nicer than Miss Faith or Miss Hope—'"

Whoever this dream lady's maid might have been that she had mistaken me for, I realized that Rory was right about "her poor mind." She wasn't dangerous. She just had times when she drifted away into that strange world of her own. As she was doing right now, looking towards the loch.

I thought I had lost her again when suddenly she smiled. "I saw you in the water, you know. I'm so glad you didn't drown. I cried and cried. I shouted at them when they wouldn't listen to me. They locked me in my room, so I had to pretend to believe them. I heard them talking. They said how could I know when it happened so far away, and I had never left the castle?"

She stopped and stamped her foot. "But I did know! I saw it just like I've always seen things, clear as clear." She held my arm in a fierce grip. "'She's still alive,' that's what the voices said. Over and over. And I was right, wasn't I?"

And releasing my arm, she began to sing softly.

There was an upward slope on the drive, and it was harder pushing the bike here than riding it. The chain came loose. Giving it all my attention, I knew I needed help.

I looked up, but she'd disappeared. And there was still a lot I wanted to know. She had called me Annie. How did she know my name?

I felt chilled. Then I realized that nice old Rory who was her friend and told her everything must have told her my name. I'd just ask her—

"Miss Charity? Hello—where are you?"

There was no reply. *Weird,* I thought. *She must have darted back into the greenery. She certainly behaves like a ghost! Appearing and disappearing!*

I heard a dog panting. Caesar and then Rory appeared around the curve in the drive. Caesar behaved in a respectful manner but wagged his tail to indicate that he knew me and I was a friend.

"Let me fix that for you," said Rory and quickly had the chain in place again.

"I think I'll walk now," I said. "Thank you. I've just met

the other sister—Miss Charity," I added.

"You were privileged. She only appears on the drive to tourists, you know." He roared with mirth. "Did she scare you?"

"Yes. But we had quite a normal chat together. Then she drifted away into the past, thought I was someone else. Is there nothing anyone can do for her?"

"Not really. She's always been like that, you know. Only one foot in the present and one in the past. Even as a little girl, she used to see things. Don't worry about her. She's quite happy. About twelve years old most of the time."

"Does she stay in the castle?" I asked.

"She has a room there. But there's an old coach house above the stables—over yonder. Those used to be the servants' quarters. And she likes to live there."

"Can she look after herself—I mean, food and so forth?"

"We see to that, Annie," he said gently. "We don't forget her although she sometimes forgets all about us. It's as if we don't exist when she's in her other world."

Poor Miss Charity.

Rory had been leading the way to the back of the castle. "I'll put the bike away for you. They'll probably want you to help out this evening. Any good at desserts? One of the visitors they've been expecting has just arrived. I saw his car parked outside the front door as I was walking Caesar."

Hurrah! That will be Mr. Jones. He must have come along the drive while I was in the village phoning Dad.

I gave a sigh of relief. My mission was almost over. Hand over the goblet, get the money, and go home to sweet old Edinburgh, to Calum again.

In the kitchen Hope was setting a silver tray for

afternoon tea. "Thank goodness, one of the guests has arrived. We'll need to have dinner this evening—"

"Excuse me—" Rory put his head around the door. "There's a man here from the phone company. Seems there's been a line down on the estate. They're doing repairs and that's why we've been having so much trouble—"

I thought about the answering machine. How could it work right when the whole system was under threat?

Hope turned around and indicated the tray. "Would you please—?" She pointed to the kettle. "Just pour the water on and take this through to the drawing room. Faith's there with Dr. Parker."

"Dr. Parker? Are you sure?" This was very interesting.

"Yes." She looked puzzled. "Why shouldn't it be Dr. Parker?"

"I wasn't sure I got his name right." I could hardly start explaining to her that I thought Dr. Parker had drowned in the loch, and it was Mr. Jones I was expecting to see.

"How long is he staying?" I asked.

"One night only. But he may wish to extend it. He has a friend with him—"

That explained the tray set for two people. I had thought Faith must be joining him.

"There's no problem. We have plenty of rooms. Come along, Rory," Hope said.

I watched them go out the door and I put the tray down again.

Dr. Parker was alive. I was delighted. So I hadn't seen his body floating in the loch dragged away by the monster. It had been fins and flippers after all and not poor Dr. Parker's arms and legs.

I felt quite weak with relief that I had been wrong. As I waited for the kettle to boil, I thought again about the events of last night.

Last night? Just half a day ago. Those horrific hours with the haunted castle on the island and the monster prowling the shore. And now today—peaceful and calm. Had I imagined it all? I wanted now to believe that I had.

As I made the tea, I thought about Dr. Parker. Would he be surprised to see me again? I wondered who his friend was—the answer obviously to where he had been since we last met. Had I also imagined the two men were chasing him? Perhaps they were just trying to sell him a holiday home.

The questions seemed to echo my footsteps as I walked down the corridor to the castle drawing room. But the most burning question of all was: what was Dr. Parker's business in Castle Roy and why this indefinite stay with his friend? Was the friend male or female?

And was this a much-needed vacation? I remembered how stressed he had been on the train and on the bus journey too. All that writing, those numbers that seemed to be worrying him.

I would soon find out. As I approached the drawing room, trying not to let my tray rattle too much, I heard the murmur of voices. Faith was rather loudly explaining the layout and history of the castle.

I opened the door. "Ah, here's Annie with your tea, sir."

His back was toward me. Over the top of the armchair I saw white hair and a hand holding spectacles as he talked. On the table beside him was an article I recognized: the red briefcase he had hugged so carefully on his travels.

"Tea! That's great. I just love afternoon tea, Mrs. Stuart."

I didn't have time to think about the voice as he swung round to face me.

"This is Dr. Parker, Annie," Faith said.

White hair, spectacles. Only it wasn't Dr. Parker. At least not the one I had traveled with. The man I set the tray in front of had a dark suit with dandruff on the collar.

Even with the change in hair color, a wig most likely, I was looking at one of the men who had been on the train, one of the two who had been chasing Dr. Parker.

They had probably murdered him and stolen his briefcase. The evidence was there before my eyes. And where was his partner in crime, the young guy with the boxer's nose who had taken such a shine to me?

Undoubtedly, he was the friend!

So where was the real Dr. Parker? Murdered, his body floating in the loch. All I had to know now was why.

Keeping well out of direct eye range, I set down the tray. I hoped Mrs. Stuart didn't expect me to pour the tea. The way my hands were shaking would certainly draw their attention. And I was fairly sure I had gone pale with shock too.

"That will do, Annie," said Faith.

I was dismissed and the bogus Dr. Parker didn't even glance in my direction. I had my head down. Maybe he didn't recognize me again. After all, maids in the castle are of little interest, and he was busy talking to Faith.

But could I stay out of his way? And his partner in crime? What would happen if—when—we came face to face and he remembered where we had met before?

I fled. I needed help. I had to talk to someone. I had gotten myself into a weird situation, pretending to be someone else. Waiting for Mr. Jones to come so that I could hand over that goblet, lying on a ledge in the chimney upstairs in the laird's study. If only I had some idea of what "Dr. Parker" was up to.

Then I remembered. The laird's lug. I would see if Rory's story about old Angus listening in to his guest's conversations in the drawing room below really worked.

I ran upstairs and closed the door. I went over to the fireplace and put my hand inside. Yes, the wooden box was still safe. And I could hear voices clearly.

Faith was apologizing for lack of staff, about it being the end of the season and so forth. She was putting on a good if not exactly truthful story. Giving him the big sell about this being a family hotel with a great tradition of hospitality.

"We pride ourselves on providing a luxury stay for a few selected guests. We never take more than twenty—"

I doubted that she would be able to manage that many. Where she and Hope slept must have been just off the kitchen. Perhaps the suites were large family rooms.

I shook my head sadly. Well, it was her problem, not mine. All I had to do was to continue my charade as a hiker looking for part-time work until Mr. Jones appeared.

"You will have our undivided attention, Dr. Parker," Faith was saying. "We do have another gentleman—"

"Will he be joining us at dinner?" Dr. Parker sounded just a bit anxious, I thought. Had I hit on the reason for his visit? Did he have business with the mysterious dealer in rare antiques, Mr. Jones?

"I do hope he will be here in time, Dr. Parker. We expect him to arrive very shortly. By helicopter, as a matter of fact." I could hear that smile. "That is another service we provide for our guests, since the hotel is so difficult to reach."

She managed a laugh that did not quite ring true to my ears. "Our guests prefer to be exclusive and many wish to be very private, if you get my meaning."

Dr. Parker murmured an agreement.

Faith was explaining that there were some small inconveniences at present. "We are having problems with our telephones."

Small problems maybe for her, but they had spelled disaster for me. If Dad had spoken to her or a real live person instead of a machine that didn't work, I would never have found myself in this tricky situation. There would have been a car to meet me, and I would never have had to spend the night risking death by freezing, by drowning, or in the jaws of the Loch Roy monster.

Dr. Parker was assuring her that it was no problem for him. He never traveled without his mobile phone.

Perhaps I could steal it and call Calum. Meanwhile, I must work out a plan while keeping well out of his way. And if we did meet, I must pretend that I did not recognize him as an impostor who had killed the professor and stolen his briefcase. I guessed it had to be very big business if it included murder.

If only I could reach Calum. He was a cop; he would know what to do in a situation involving murder. The crime squad was where he went to work every day. There was only one thing to do: get to Rory's phone or head for the village and call Calum.

I was about to leave when I heard the drawing room door open. Someone had come in. I heard Dr. Parker's voice, "Ah, Mrs. Stuart. This is my partner, Mr. Fry."

"Pleased to meet you, Mrs. Stuart."

"I'll show you to your rooms—"

The voices faded as they walked to the door.

The second villain, the young guy who had wanted to follow me, had arrived. Between them they had murdered the real Dr. Parker. They were ruthless killers and whatever their reason for being here, it spelled danger— not only for me but for everyone else at Castle Roy.

The smell of death was in the air.

CHAPTER
13

As I went downstairs, a
delicious smell of cooking came from the kitchen area.
It reminded me that I had eaten very little since leaving
Edinburgh. I had put aside all thoughts of being hungry
in the excitement of the last few hours. Now I knew that
before I did anything else I must eat—and soon.

In the kitchen Hope and Rory were talking to the man
from the telephone company. I could see by their faces
that it wasn't good news. He was being very gloomy
about the answering machine on the table.

Hope looked up. "Everything all right, Annie?"

"Fine," I said as I wandered over to the cooker. "May I
have some soup?"

"Help yourself."

I did and took a second bowl unasked—it tasted so
good. I felt much better. I could see things clearer now.
My brain had been starved and needed feeding. Perhaps

a couple of bowls of soup inside me and several slices of freshly baked bread would give me some of the answers I needed just now.

I gathered that the Stuarts were discussing the new answering machine. Theirs was old and they had bought it secondhand in Inverness. The salesman was giving them a hard sell on their new system. More instruments in a place this size, a phone in every bedroom, more bells were needed. *And more money for the phone company,* I thought.

"See you this evening, Hope," said Rory. "And while I'm in Inverness seeing my sister, I'll just take a look at some of the shops, see what they have to offer."

As for me, I was no nearer to sorting out my own problem. If I warned the Stuarts that Dr. Parker was an impostor, then I had to tell them who I was. If, as I suspected, the killers were here to do a deal with Mr. Jones and they found out about the goblet, what then? They would surely wait to rob the man from Edinburgh too!

Faith came in looking pleased until the phone man, about to leave, greeted her with the words, "You'll be out of touch until they fix the power lines up the hill."

"And what are we supposed to do until then?" she asked.

"The phones in the village are still working, madam." He leaned forward. "As I was telling Miss Stuart, you wouldn't have any of these problems if you would invest in a mobile phone. Think it over. Here's my card. 'Bye now."

"This is awful," said Faith. "What are we going to do?"

"We'll just keep hoping that we don't have an emergency till the lines are fixed."

"How long are the new guests staying?" I asked.

"Just passing through. I've left it open for a couple of days. We have plenty of room, Annie, but it is never good policy to let guests know that the hotel is empty. Bad for business, you know. So keep it to yourself if they ask you. Hint that we are usually very busy at this time of year."

Listening to Hope and Faith, I began to have second thoughts. Perhaps the killers' visit had nothing to do with Mr. Jones. As far as the Stuarts knew, he was coming to meet a gentleman from Edinburgh. "Parker" had not hinted to Faith that he was interested in Mr. Jones. Or were they all in it together, their meeting at Castle Roy made to look accidental? I had to find out.

"Transportation is very difficult in this area," Faith was saying. "It's fortunate that we have enough room on the front drive out there for a helicopter to land. That's how Mr. Jones will be traveling. Many of our rich guests prefer it. Others like to come across the loch by boat. It's more romantic that way."

As she talked, my mind was elsewhere. How was I to warn Mr. Jones when he landed that Dr. Parker was a phony? Somehow I had to get him aside and warn him of a fraud. I had to tell him who I was. Thoughts tumbled through my head at an alarming rate, like the fast forward on a videotape.

Hope appeared at the door. "I've saddled the pony cart. I'm off to collect supplies that Len left."

Faith looked at me. "Rory has the van. Annie could give you a hand."

"Good idea," said Hope, and I couldn't think of any excuse to refuse.

I had to get in touch with Calum, and some opportunity might arise.

Outside, what Hope had described as a pony cart was waiting. Only it was pulled by a horse, and it looked like something from a Western movie about pioneering days.

I was quite delighted. This was an adventure. As I sat up front with Hope and we jogged along, I realized what a short distance it was to the loch. When you knew the way, that is. It was a warm, calm day and even my old enemy the Highland beast looked quite harmless in his field.

A young man was anchoring Len's boat as we reached the shed where the supplies were left. "This is Len's nephew," Hope explained. "He comes over to visit sometimes."

He grinned. "Have you heard the news?" We hadn't.

"It was on TV this morning. We're on the map at last. There's been a old man washed up at Corriedon. At the edge of the loch. It's all roped off—I couldn't get away. The police were there questioning everyone."

"How awful. Do they know who it is?"

"No, he's a stranger. But according to Jock, he was on the bus from Glenmohr when it broke down at Corriedon. There was a young woman with him. They were heading this way, and he thinks they maybe borrowed Baird's old rowboat to cut across the loch. Anyway, they can't have got very far. The boat's been washed up—well and truly wrecked."

I could hear my heart thumping as Hope said, "Tourists, were they?"

"That's what Jock thinks. They're dragging the loch for the woman's body now."

"What a terrible thing to happen," said Hope as the boy helped us load the supplies into the cart.

"Aye, it is that. Must get back to see if they've got the body yet. There was quite a crowd gathered when I left." He sounded quite excited by this rare event.

As we trotted back to the castle, Hope was full of ideas. None of them were anywhere near the truth. "I wonder who they were."

I could have told her then that the man was the real professor, not the man she knew as Dr. Parker. I could have told her who the girl was too. Except that I was supposed to be drowned. And in my present dangerous situation, I thought it wise to stay that way.

In the kitchen, I helped Hope unload the supplies.

"Tomatoes!" she said. "I particularly asked for fresh tomatoes. Things for the salad tonight. There's a man in the village, just beside the shop, sells them from his greenhouse." She looked at me. "Would you—?"

I needed no better excuse to go down and phone Calum. "Of course," I said.

I went up to old Angus's room to get my purse. I'd need plenty of coins for that pay phone. My tiny window above the drawing room looked down on the front drive. There was a car parked, a sticker on the windscreen from a car rental in Inverness. What had happened to the white Ford?

I was very nervous about that goblet. The longer I had it, the worse I got. So I decided to check once more to make sure it was safe inside the chimney.

As I leaned forward I heard voices, clear as if they were in the same room. Then I remembered the "laird's lug." I was overhearing the killers, I could smell their cigar smoke, and they were speaking about me.

The young thug Mr. Fry said, "Of course, I knew her. What's she doing here, anyway? How much does she know?"

"Probably nothing for us to worry about. She was just looking for work."

"What about Parker?"

There was a harsh laugh. "No need to worry about him. He's not likely to bother us again."

"But the girl—" Fry insisted. "She was on the train with him and she seemed mighty interested in him. We don't know how much he told her."

"He wouldn't talk to her. He was on the run, remember?

All we have to do is keep our cool. Give the briefcase to Jones, get the money, and get away fast."

There was a laugh from Fry. "That case was a stroke of genius. A real bonus. And if there's going to be any trouble from these folk, we can deal with that too," he said grimly, but he sounded worried.

"It'll be all right," said Parker. "I've done it all before. You're new to this—"

"Come on! I worked with him in the laboratory. I knew what the formula would be worth to a rival chemical company in the States. About a million bucks!"

"But not as much as the Duke of Windsor's briefcase here."

I heard the case click open.

"We were lucky he took it everywhere with him. Considering the prices small items go for at the New York auction, this will be worth a fortune to the right person. And the contents too. Parker's father was butler to the Duke for years. There are letters—"

"Have you read them?" asked Fry eagerly.

"No need. Just look at the signatures. There are all sorts of things that went on that Parker's old man knew about."

"Pity we had to kill him."

"Come off it. Too late for remorse. There was no other way we were going to get him to hand over the formula and the case."

"You wouldn't have known about Jones or had this contact if it hadn't been for me. I found that out for you too, don't forget." There was a hint of menace in Fry's voice.

A moment of silence, then he asked: "Any idea who he's working for?"

"No one knows that," said "Parker." "He says that he's a confidential agent for auctioneers—" The case snapped shut and I missed the name.

But Fry whistled. "The top one! We should get a good price there. If Jones is for real."

"Who cares who he's working for as long as he delivers the money."

I had heard enough. So Jones was the reason for their being here. And it sounded as if he might be a crook too. Or perhaps he was like my father—in the same trade and using a false name. Knowing Dad's shady business deals, that wouldn't have surprised me.

Should it even concern me? All I had to do was hand over the goblet. I'd warn Jones what they were up to and get him to take me back with him in the helicopter. That was my way out. Like something from a James Bond movie.

Brilliant! But there was more to it—my conscience took over. I couldn't let them get away with murdering the professor.

That was for the crime squad to deal with, the department of Detective Sergeant Calum Crail. Wouldn't he be pleased that I had enough evidence to convict the killers?

I realized, of course, that the Edinburgh police force couldn't operate in the Highlands, but murder was murder. Calum would know what to do. There would be a great amount of red tape to be cut, phones buzzing and computers consulted before they could come to my aid. On second thought, I had better take that helicopter ride, even if it meant missing the final scene with "Parker" and Fry in handcuffs.

But alas, Fate had another plan. I was never to make that walk to the village or the phone call to Calum.

CHAPTER 14

Calum's Story

I had just seen the VIPs off at Edinburgh Airport in one of the planes of the Queen's flight. The red carpet was being rolled up as I was making my way to my car.

I thought I'd stop and buy a newspaper. Waiting in line to pay for it, I glanced at the Scottish news on the television monitor. Instead of the usual political stuff, there was a big story.

"A body has been found near Loch Ness, on the Corriedon side of Loch Roy. Police divers are investigating the possibility that two people were involved—"

I froze. From the road map of the area Annie and I had looked at together, I remembered that Castle Roy was across the loch from Corriedon.

Of course, Annie should have left, on her way home by now. But I couldn't shake off a terrible feeling of disaster. I wanted to hear more about the body they'd recovered, but there was too much noise around me from the airport.

I got into my car and drove as fast as I could, but I was in the thick of the commuter traffic heading for home. The traffic had never seemed slower moving, red lights everywhere, lines of cars in front and behind.

I swore. Dare I put on the siren, get the police lights flashing, get priority? I knew that was crazy even to think about. What if I was stopped by a patrol officer and asked what was my hurry? If I had to tell them it was a private matter, that I was worried about my girlfriend, my head would be on the block. I'd just been promoted, after all, and that was the surest way back to walking a beat.

As we stopped at yet another red light, I told myself not to be an idiot. Think straight! Why should Annie be involved? A body in a loch near where she was heading? Most probably a boating accident. Why should I presume that this one was murder? If only I could have heard properly.

I went straight to Hamish Kelty's bookshop. It was closed so I rang the house bell. The outside door clicked and I ran up the spiral stairs. He took a while to let me in.

"Have you seen the news?" I panted.

"No. Is it worth looking at?" he said, switching on the TV. It was too late for the news, of course. "Calum, what's wrong?"

While he began setting the table, I told him what I had seen on the TV at the airport.

He looked surprised. "Oh, that! Yes, I heard it on the radio."

"That's near where Annie is—"

"Was," he said. "She should be on her way home by now."

"When did you hear from her?" I asked.

"This morning. She asked me to contact you, but I didn't have any luck—"

I had been guarding the VIPs all day.

"Our client was due by helicopter. Annie was leaving straight after making the delivery. Nothing to worry about, Calum. You'll be seeing her in an hour or two."

"I suppose you're right."

"Of course I'm right. Look, I'll get her to call you as soon as she arrives."

He didn't seem very concerned about Annie. He seemed ill at ease, anxious to get rid of me. In anyone else but Annie's father, his behavior would have been classed as suspicious. As if he didn't want me making too many inquiries or too much spotlight directed on his client and Annie's reason for being at Castle Roy.

But the next moment I knew the answer. Susie came out of the bedroom. She was fully dressed and had a kind of glow about her. It gave me an idea that my visit had interrupted something. Not that I'm prim about such things. Just envious. I wished it were Annie and me.

In my office at the station, I tried calling the castle. I was told by the operator that the lines on the estate were being repaired. All phones in the area were out of order. If I cared to leave my number, they would call me as soon as normal services were resumed.

In my official role as D.S. Crail, I put through a call to the Scene of Accident Inquiry at Corriedon.

"The body? It's that of an elderly man. No ID. Age and name unknown as yet," I was told.

I sighed with relief. At least it wasn't my Annie.

"Have you information to help us with our inquiry, sarge?" I was asked.

"No. It isn't one of the missing persons on our lists. How long has he been in the water?"

"We're still waiting for the forensic report," he replied.

"Any clues of your own as to how it happened?" I asked, trying to sound mildly interested.

"It wasn't accidental drowning, if that's what you mean. There are head injuries and we'll be treating this as murder," he added grimly.

I put down the phone. It hadn't anything to do with Annie. I should have been shouting with joy. But knowing her, I had a gut feeling that if there was a chance to get involved in a murder, then my Annie would plunge in with both feet. I got my answer to what I dreaded most shortly afterwards.

The police computer works fast. Press a few keys and I had up-to-date, strictly private information about any crimes in a twenty-mile radius of Loch Roy.

I sat with the map, working it all out. Some vandals had destroyed a phone box. (That might be a clue to the phone company's headaches.) Two drunk and disorderly fights. A dog missing. A battered wife . . .

And then. A doctor reported having his car stolen from Glenmohr. I stopped to think. The only thing that might be a link with Annie was that Corriedon was on the road to Lochroy.

Dr. Burns was in general practice near Inverness. I sat back and thought about that. It was a long shot, but this stolen vehicle just might have been used as the murderer's getaway car.

I got his number. Luckily, I caught him as he was leaving his office. I said I was from the police and it was in connection with the theft of his car. He was very willing to tell me all about it. It was a white Ford. I wrote down the registration number.

"How did it happen, doctor?" I asked.

"I go to my office at Glenmohr once a week. The people around there are pretty healthy, except for farm accidents, of course. So they don't need a resident doctor. After my office hours I look in on my elderly house-bound patients. I have quite a few; they live to a great age in that area," he added proudly. "These are mostly social calls. They don't need medicals but it cheers them up to know they are being looked after."

"So the thieves broke into your car and drove it away?" I asked.

"Not quite like that." There was a small silence. "They didn't need to do that. I'd left the keys in it. That's quite usual. Nobody ever locks their cars—or their doors—in Glenmohr. It's a law-abiding, peaceful place. They all know each other."

I was thinking about the strangers they didn't know as he continued, "First I knew that it had been stolen was an indignant phone call from old Mr. Bell. He's 98 and still works a farm near Corriedon. I keep an eye on his heart and he's a grand old man who loves a gossip. Well, he'd seen my car—the most well-known in Glenmohr—flash past his farm. He was out feeding the pigs at the time. He thought I had forgotten all about my weekly visit and his indigestion tablets. He was very cross.

"They still haven't found the car. I'll be lucky if I ever see it again," Dr. Burns said sadly. "All they do is change the number plates, go to a big town, and make a quick sale."

"Was it vandals—joyriders?"

"Oh, no. I went to the gas station to see if I could borrow a car or if Billy would drive me home. When I told him about my car, he said he thought he knew who had stolen it. While he was changing a tire, two men rushed after the school bus for Lochroy. The driver refused to stop for them."

None of this was consoling. The school bus was the one Annie was supposed to be catching.

"So these two men rushed over to the garage, all out of breath and absolutely furious," Dr. Burns continued. "They wanted to hire a car from Billy, but he doesn't have rental cars. How about the one he was working on? He said that belonged to a customer. Imagine the cheek of them!

"Well, to cut a long story short, Billy didn't like the look of these two men, one young, one middle-aged. Maybe he watches too many crime movies, but he was sure they were carrying guns."

Crooks carrying guns—oh, God! That sounded just like something Annie would get messed up in!

"Anyway, they had a desperate look about them. And Billy swears he saw them staring across the road at my car sitting outside my office. Ten minutes later when he came out of the garage, it had gone. He reckons they stole it."

Thanking Dr. Burns for his help, I said we'd do what we could to recover his car. Then I called the Scene of Accident Inquiry at Corriedon again to report my conversation with the doctor. That was old news for them, but it gave me a chance to ask a few more questions.

"Any more info on the drowned man?" I asked.

"As a matter of fact, there is. The driver of the school bus has identified the body. Thinks it was one of his passengers on the bus that broke down in Corriedon yesterday. There was a young woman traveling with the old guy and they were heading for Lochroy. When the bus broke down, they maybe tried to get across the loch in an old rowboat. It was washed up as well. They're looking for the woman's body right now."

Annie—oh, Annie!

End of Calum's Story

CHAPTER 15

I was a prisoner in Castle Roy. Gagged and tied to a chair in old Angus's study, helpless as a trussed up chicken.

I suppose I should have been grateful that was all Fry had done to me when they followed me upstairs. Jones's helicopter had just landed. I heard Parker say they should be getting on with the business at hand, now that I was out of their way.

I shuddered. I could do nothing to warn Mr. Jones. The two killers had decided that I knew too much. They could have gotten rid of me right away. Parker had been holding a gun to my head when Fry reminded him that bodies are a problem.

That probably saved my life. Fry said he had a soft heart. "Such a shame to waste her. Let's keep her around until later," he said. The look on Parker's face as he put away the gun told a very different story.

I hadn't a clue to what was going on downstairs. I could hear distant voices and sounds, but why, oh, why didn't they come into the drawing room where I could hear every word from the "laird's lug"?

How were Faith and Hope dealing with the situation downstairs? Were they wondering what had happened to me? Or had the killers given them some plausible story about seeing me leaving the castle? They would just shrug and go on with their work. Typical of young people these days, they would think.

I thought at first that Parker and Fry might have finished the deal with Jones and had taken the chance to disappear in the helicopter. I learned later that was their intention. However, the pilot refused to take them off immediately and shouted that he would be back later.

Mr. Jones then told them one of the main reasons for his visit was to collect a rare and precious goblet for a client in New York. That was a mistake. The two greedy men then decided to wait for the arrival of Mr. Jones's Edinburgh gentleman with the goblet.

Then they would have the professor's stolen formula, the Duke of Windsor's briefcase, and a priceless historic goblet! However, they were getting impatient, nervous about the delays, and wondering what had happened to the seller Jones was supposed to meet. They didn't realize that the goblet was resting in the chimney above their heads!

If only I could escape from my bonds. There wasn't much chance of either of them coming to old Angus's study. And Mr. Jones would be in one of the guest bedrooms on the other side of the house.

If only Faith or Hope would come into the drawing room. But even if I hadn't been gagged, the "laird's lug" operated one-way only. It was like an old-fashioned ear-trumpet. If they came into the drawing room, I could hear every word they said, but they couldn't hear me. Unless I threw something down the chimney to attract their attention, they would never know I was all tied up, a prisoner in the tiny room above their heads.

I considered my bonds. They had used an old, frayed curtain cord to hastily tie me up. I tested it and had a good feeling that it wasn't very strong. With luck, since my wrists were very thin, I might work one hand free.

It would soon be dark and I was getting frantic. I had to escape before Parker and Fry put two and two together. I had been traveling in this direction along with the professor, so I could be the person with the goblet Jones was waiting for. Or I might have some vital information on its delivery.

Wriggling my wrists against a nail in the chair was very painful, but I had to try. I found I had been right about the condition of the cord. I felt it loosen and tear enough to squeeze my wrist through. A few more tugs and I was free. I pulled the gag off my mouth and wondered what to do next. There was no key in the door, so they hadn't been able to lock me in. Cautiously I crept downstairs.

How was I to get out of the castle unseen? I listened carefully. There was no one in the drawing room. They would all be at dinner. I could hear voices and the cheerful clink of cutlery. Maybe I could slip past them and into the kitchen. But I would have to go past the dining room, and its door was open. I could not risk it, even to reach the phone in the kitchen.

Calling the police takes time and I hadn't any to waste explaining it all to the Stuarts. I'm sure Faith wouldn't believe the story of a hitchhiker looking for work against the story of a paying guest.

In fact, the less the Stuarts knew, the safer they would

be. I thought of Rory. He should be back from Inverness by now. Maybe I could go out the front door and use Rory's phone.

When I reached the front door, opening it was no simple matter, for it creaked like a mad thing. Did no one in this house know anything about oiling hinges? I tried a few more inches and the noise it made would have wakened the dead.

I squeezed through and I was out at last, the cold night air on my face, running down the steps. I must get to Rory! But I was too late. Someone had heard the front door open and raised the alarm.

I saw Fry on the front steps. And he had seen me. I couldn't run to the kennels now. If Rory wasn't home yet, then I would be trapped indeed. I had to get to the village.

I started to run. I hadn't gone far when I knew Fry was gaining on me. With two good ankles, I could have outrun him, but I knew I'd never make it now.

I would have to take cover and try to lose him. I leapt off the drive and began to weave my way through the trees. I flattened myself against one of them, hoping he would pass me by, but I wasn't quick enough.

"Got you!" He grabbed me. I screamed and struggled, kicked out at him.

It was useless. He had me in a firm grip and he laughed. "We have some unfinished business, remember? You aren't going anywhere and I'm not needed back there. So let's get on with it."

His mouth covered mine and his hands roved. I wanted to be sick as he threw me on the ground.

Suddenly there was a bloodcurdling moan—not my own. A greenish figure appeared in the twilight. A tall and ghostly figure of a woman in a flowing gown and a huge picture hat. She pointed at him and came slowly forward.

Taken completely by surprise, he gave a yelp of horror. He had to let me go to reach for his gun.

That was all I needed. I kicked his wrist. The gun fell onto the grass and I made a grab for it. He lurched forward and Charity tripped him up very neatly. I hit him over the head with the gun, and he fell like a sack of potatoes.

I thought I had probably killed him, but I was sure I could plead self-defense. I had other worries right then. "I was on my way to the village to phone for the police. He's a killer. He and his partner murdered a man they pulled out of the loch at Corriedon this morning."

Charity nodded, but I wasn't sure how much she was taking in. She was staring, fascinated, at the gun. "Give me that," she said. "I'll see that he doesn't get away." I handed it to her. "I've always wanted to use one of these," she said, lovingly weighing it in her hand.

He wasn't moving. I told her, "I think he's dead."

"And good riddance too," she said cheerfully. "Off you go."

"Thanks, Charity," I said and took to my heels.

I hoped I could trust her but I hadn't many options. I soon found out that it was a mistake and I should never have left her. A pistol shot!

I hesitated. Should I go back? Charity might be hurt!

But it was Fry who staggered through the bushes.

I ran. The gates were in sight. I was almost there when my ankle gave out once again. Fry knocked me savagely to the ground.

There was no escape this time as a fist crashed into my face. Blue lights danced above my head and faded away as I fainted.

CHAPTER 16

"Annie!"

I wasn't dead after all. My chin hurt. I opened my eyes.

"Annie, love. You have to stop making a habit of this."

The dearest voice in the whole world. I was lying in the back of a police car with Calum's arms around me.

The blue flashing lights lit up the drive as we stopped in front of the castle.

"I'll be back. Don't go away." A quick kiss and he was gone. I saw him again among the black-clad figures of armed cops racing up the steps to the front door.

A police helicopter was parked on the drive.

Ten minutes later it was all over. From the dining room window, we watched Parker and Fry being marched down the steps and into the police cars.

Faith, Hope, Charity, and me. Charity was still in her grey gown and very unghostlike. She was downing a second very large gin and tonic and gloating over her part in the capture of two crooks.

She kept repeating how sorry she was that she had failed—that she hadn't killed Fry instead of just grazing his shoulder.

"It was only a flesh wound," she said sadly. Then she brightened and smiled at us all. "Not bad for a first shot. I think I had better get some practice in, though."

Mr. Jones joined us. He was bewildered and a little uneasy about all that had happened. Silent in the midst of all the excitement, he was still waiting patiently for the Edinburgh gentleman to show up with his goblet. Although I studied him several times, later I couldn't give anyone an exact description. All I remember was a small man of anonymous age and appearance, perhaps the best qualification for his job!

Later I learned from Calum what the police computer had told him. The fake Dr. Parker who had taken the professor's place after killing him was a well-known criminal. His real name (or one of them) was Warner, and he was wanted for a number of crimes, including murder.

Fry was a small-time crook who had worked in the professor's laboratory. He knew about the secret chemical formula and that Dr. Parker was being blackmailed by a colleague's wife about an early association with the Russian KGB.

"Wait a minute—the professor, you say, and a colleague's wife?"

"Yes. They'd had an affair long ago."

"Well, that surprises me. I didn't think he had it in him."

Calum grinned. "He had been one of the good guys,

Annie, but there were two things he couldn't resist: power and money. They go together and lead to disaster. His father had worked for the Duke of Windsor when he was King Edward—before he abdicated to marry Mrs. Simpson. According to Parker, the Duke gave him this briefcase as a parting gift."

He pointed to it lying on the table.

"I knew that." I told Calum how I had listened in old Angus's study from the "laird's lug." I had overheard the two crooks in the drawing room talking about the briefcase.

"Mr. Jones wants to buy it. The money will go to the professor's son and daughter. It will be almost like winning the National Lottery for them."

"What about the chemical formula?" I asked.

Calum shook his head. "Jones wouldn't touch anything like that." He grinned. "At least not officially. It is stolen goods, you know. Even if the professor discovered it, legally it belongs to the college he was working for."

Since I had never managed to phone Calum, it seemed like nothing short of a miracle that he was here beside me. "How on earth did you get here?" I asked.

He grinned. "Easy. I did my bit of Sherlock Holmes, courtesy of the computer," said Calum.

He told me about tracking down the doctor at Glenmohr. He explained that people thought the professor and I had taken off in a boat, which later washed up on the shore wrecked.

He held my hand very tightly. "Never in my life do I want to go through all that again, Annie. I really thought you were gone forever. I knew nothing else mattered but coming here. Even if it meant handing in my stripes, I had to find you.

"Luckily, I have a very human and understanding Inspector. When I told him, he said, 'Well done, Crail. Good work. You've helped further our inquiries. Now I think it's up to you to go up there personally and finish the job. I'll put it right with the Inverness police and, as time is of the essence, we might manage a helicopter.'"

He looked at his watch. "That was just a couple of hours ago."

"But I still don't know how you found out what was happening here at the castle. The phones aren't working."

"They are now. There's nothing like the law and police business to get things buzzing." He stopped and listened. "And if I'm not mistaken there's Mr. Jones's helicopter, come back to collect him. I'll leave you to do the honors, Annie. Put him out of his misery."

I took the wooden box from its hiding place in the chimney and went into the drawing room. Mr. Jones was looking out of the window.

Quickly I explained and he laughed, "So you are the gentleman from Edinburgh everyone has been waiting for!"

He opened the box and lovingly held the goblet in his hands. Holding it up to the light, I had to admit it was very beautiful. I felt quite quite proud of myself for having preserved this piece of Scottish history through hell and high water!

"I thought it was better to stay silent until I could hand it over to you in safety," I explained.

"Quite right, my dear. For the safe delivery of this goblet, you risked a lot of things, including your own life. Your father should be very proud of his daughter. In fact, we all owe you a great deal. Great to do business with you. Give this to your father—and thank you."

The sealed envelope was heavy. I had expected a check, not cash. As I put it in my backpack, he noticed my hesitation.

"It's all there. Count it if you wish."

"No. I trust you, Mr. Jones."

I should have known it was part of Dad's business deals that he never dealt in checks. He wanted ready cash. There were very good reasons for this. Although I decided Jones was probably an honest man, not all of Dad's dealings were honest.

I explained to Calum that Dad is old-fashioned about money: he prefers dealing in pounds sterling rather than any foreign currency.

*   *   *

We had quite a celebration that evening. I got the chance to have a bath and wash my hair—in a modern and luxurious guest bathroom. And I had occasion to wear the little black dress. Looking at my reflection as I went downstairs, I felt that Dad and Susie would have been proud of me.

The Stuarts were so grateful. They couldn't do enough to make us feel at home. They insisted that we had saved their lives and that the castle was ours to enjoy as long as we wished to stay.

I looked at Calum and he said, "Well, thank you. I have some calls to make, but maybe we could stay for the weekend. If that suits you, Annie."

It did indeed. I thought of one of those lovely suites of rooms upstairs with a four-poster bed. And so did Calum.

*   *   *

As we walked by the loch the next morning, there were Rory and Caesar. Caesar took one look at Calum and wagged his tail, overjoyed to sniff out a true dog lover. There was much patting of heads and shaking of paws. I watched it all with Rory—from a safe distance. Calum thought Caesar was great. He and Rory talked dogs for a while.

When Len appeared in his boat with the Stuarts' supplies, he wanted to hear all the news. "Nothing like this has ever happened in Corriedon before." He sighed. "I doubt if it will ever happen again in my lifetime. Good for the tourist trade, though," he added.

Len was delighted to meet a real detective from Edinburgh, and I had a feeling we weren't going to get much walking that morning. I had an idea. "Calum would love to see the island. He loves old ruins."

Len seemed to find this confession surprising for a policeman. "Great! Look, I'll take you across—"

"That's very kind, but how do we get back? No rowboat this time," I said.

"I'll collect you. In an hour's time, say. Meanwhile I'll have a drink up at the castle. I want to hear all the gory details from Faith."

*   *   *

Calum thought the old castle was great. And although I thought it was one of the saddest places I had ever seen, it was just sad, not scary at all by daylight. I told Calum all about that terrible night, seeing the monster in the loch.

He said, "You realize, of course, that what you saw was poor old Dr. Parker's dead body."

I shook my head. "No, Calum. I saw it twice. It had a head, a neck—"

I looked over the water. I could hardly believe my eyes.

"Look, over there, Calum—there it is again! Now will you believe me?"

Calum looked and then he laughed. "Annie, one of the first things you should do when we get back home is have your eyes tested."

"There's nothing wrong with my eyes. I have perfect sight," I protested.

We were still arguing when Len came back to collect us. I was trying to convince Calum that what I had seen was the monster of Loch Roy.

As Len set us ashore, Rory was walking along the path with Caesar shaking the water off himself. "Keep away, Caesar. You'll drown everybody."

I remembered Rory saying that Caesar loved to swim, that he couldn't keep him out of water. Why hadn't that occurred to me at the time? And now I had another thought—

"We saw him from the island," said Calum. "Annie thought she was seeing the monster."

Rory smiled shyly as he stared across the loch. If it hadn't been for all that face hair, I am sure we would have seen the blush that slowly rose from his neck.

But Calum knew. "Well done, Rory. Great for the tourist trade."

I wasn't convinced. I'm still sure that what I saw that night was not a dog. Charity knew it too. And so perhaps did the Stuarts, but dogs are more easy to train to make appearances when they are needed. Monsters are not guaranteed to pop up in the tourist season. Or when they were most wanted, to prove my point.

The loch was as smooth as glass, the sun shone, and our weekend at Castle Roy was sheer bliss. We promised the Stuarts we would definitely come back on our honeymoon.

When we were leaving, Rory insisted we come in to the kennels for a drink. "Make it coffee," said Calum. "I'm driving a police car." Rory thought that was a great laugh.

As Rory went into the kitchen to put on the kettle, still chatting to us, Calum was looking at one of the old photographs on the wall. The same one I had been looking at when I had used Rory's phone to call Dad.

A group of servants was sitting on the front steps of the castle. There was something about the photo that had haunted me. I had never found out exactly why, but it left me with a strange feeling that touched some chord of memory.

But what? The maids were wearing white aprons and caps. Some of the men were dressed like waiters or butlers. These were the indoor servants, what Edinburgh folks referred to as "in high service." There were other men wearing caps, tweeds, and boots—outdoor servants, workers on the estate.

The castle in the background still looked the same, except there was no ivy creeping up the walls. It was a happy photograph taken in summer sunshine, but there was something sad too. It belonged to a time when the Stuarts could live grandly and still afford a staff of servants. Before their fortunes changed and they had to take in paying guests and be servants themselves.

There was a feeling of the remote past about the photograph, as if it had been taken a very long time ago.

Calum was studying it closely. He just loves old photographs and collects historic ones of Edinburgh and the early police force. He has albums of groups dating way back to the 1880s.

"Those were the days, Annie," he said wistfully.

"For some folks," I said, remembering Charity's words.

"If you had tons of money and you were one of the gentry. But not if you had to carry jugs of hot water up great flights of stairs to icy bedrooms. Or the slop pails to empty every morning and the fires to light at six o'clock on a dark morning."

Calum grinned. "You seem to know all about it."

"I've read books. There was this one—"

But Calum wasn't listening. Suddenly he took my arm. "Look at this guy, Annie," he said, pointing to a man in the front row. "Notice anything about him?" He sounded excited. "No? Surely you know who he looks like!"

The smiling face, the thick, curly hair were a bit familiar, but I couldn't think where I'd seen them before. I shook my head.

"Come on, Annie. That man's the image of your father. I mean it! Look again. It could be him when he was young!"

I laughed. "He's not that old!"

Rory came in with coffee. He saw us both looking at the photo.

"We're just admiring the good old days," Calum said. "When was this one taken?"

Rory laughed. "Not all that long ago. I'm in that picture. There, in the back row."

A young Rory, clean-shaven. I'd never have known him.

Calum pointed: "That guy in the front? Who was he?"

Rory put on his glasses, stared at the group, and scratched his head. "You have me there. He wasn't one of us. I mean, he wasn't one of the Stuart servants. He was a brainy young chap, a schoolteacher. Come up during vacation to help out with the grouse beaters over the moors. The beaters went out to scare the grouse from where they were hiding. Then the hunters came along to shoot the grouse. A lot of young Highland lads came home in the summer, especially if they needed a bit of extra money. The Stuarts used to pay the beaters well. Grouse hunting was quite a sport here."

Rory paused and looked at the photo again. "I wish I could remember his name. That girl he's got his arm around. Now it comes back to me. He was crazy about her. She was one of the servants."

He looked at me. "I remember her name though. It was Annie—same as you." He smiled. "Funny thing. When I first saw you, I thought you looked like her."

Someone else had thought that too. And that solved the puzzle of how Charity knew my name. Rory had told her, and she had got it all confused in her mind with the servant girl she had been so fond of. The one who was kind and had cared for her.

"She was Miss Charity's maid," Rory explained. "Charity was real upset when she went off with that fellow and married him. It was a mistake, as it turned out."

"How a mistake?" I asked.

"Well, it wasn't a happy marriage from what we heard. Annie was pretty and good-natured, but she couldn't keep up with her schoolteacher man's grand ideas. She was an ordinary Highland girl, you understand. She had no education to speak of. She should have married some local lad. She had offers enough."

"What happened to them?" I said.

"They went to live in some remote village over on the west coast. Stormer, I think it was. Miss Charity tried to keep in touch with her." He sighed. "But it was a tragedy. The marriage didn't last long. She died, poor girl."

Calum was getting anxious. He looked at his watch. He wanted to get home before dark. "I'll just check the car," he said, his polite way of telling me to cut it short. "I think we'll need to get more gas."

"How did she die?" I asked.

Rory shook his head. "Who knows? We never found out, except that— well, it wasn't illness or a natural death, if you know what I mean. Something they didn't want to speak about."

"Miss Charity told me she saw her in the water, but that she didn't drown," I explained.

Rory sighed. "Miss Charity believes she has the Sight. That she can see all sorts of things that none of the rest of us are aware of. She gets warnings and so forth. They've always caused a lot of trouble because she never sees good things coming." He shook his head sadly.

Calum hadn't said a word. Now he asked, "What became of the schoolteacher?"

"He left the Highlands. Just disappeared. There was a baby, I think. He took the baby with him. Nobody ever heard of them again."

I was very silent all the way back to Edinburgh. I tried to sound interested in Calum's plans for the future, for our future. I tried to sound excited about getting married soon. When we reached the Royal Mile, I ran up the spiral stairs and hugged and kissed Dad. I knew I was glad to be home safe and sound, but my mind was already busy elsewhere.

Next morning the mail brought a fat check from Mr. Jones. Addressed to me personally, the note said, "A small bonus. With my gratitude."

"A nice wedding present," said Dad.

But by then I had plans of my own. Secret plans I wasn't ready to discuss with my father or with Calum. I was going to Stormer. I was going to find out what happened to my mother.

To find out how she had died. And to find out if I had killed her. Or to find out if she was still alive.